Praise for the Rocky Bluff P.D. Mystery Series...

Full of suspense, realistic, and sprinkled with a light touch of romance, *Smell of Death* by F.M. Meredith is a sure hit for crime fiction fans...an engaging, well-written, and gripping page turner, that will leave you hungry for the next book in the Rocky Bluff P.D. series.
— **Cheryl Malandrinos, The Book Connection**

"...The police work in *Smell of Death* is not fancy, or even particularly high-tech. There's no CSI magic to be found here. There are no courtroom theatrics, and no hyper-intuitive detectives. Just hard working cops doing the sort of methodical spadework that probably solves most real life crimes.

Fans of *Hill Street Blues* will find this book right up their alley. F. M. Meredith has crafted a smoothly compelling police drama, peopled by convincing characters." —**Jeff Edwards, AAA Book Reviews**

"...The nuts and bolts of a police procedural are woven seamlessly with the involvement of the major characters in a number of sub-plots playing out over what amounts to about two weeks in Rocky Bluff. It makes for what is simply a great read—with enough twists and turns to avoid being predictable, and with characters you will continue to think about after the mysteries are solved. Leaving hope, of course, that another Rocky Bluff PD story will find its way out of Marilyn's active imagination very soon!"– **Claudia Elliott, Editor, Southern Sierra Messenger Express!**

"In the style of the best of Wambaugh, albeit with a gentler hand and less rugged language, F. M. Meredith draws characters we want to know better, those with whom we'd like to kick back and share a beer. She lays bare their flaws and weaknesses while showing us that these brave men and women, who risk their lives to protect us on a daily basis, are really no different than we are-decent, caring individuals with the same hardships and triumphs, struggling to do their best as husbands and wives, and moms and dads, while keeping their humanity. The members of the Rocky Bluff P. D. are definitely folks I want to visit again, and look forward to "riding along" as they guarantee the triumph of justice over evil." **Miqui Miller, MySpace.com**

"...The saga opens with a daughter and mother murder. Both happened on the same night, but in different locations. Though Stacey believes these murders are related, evidence and a motive will have to be found. In the meantime, a little girl disappears, there's arson to investigate and a rash of burglaries all keep Rocky Bluff's finest busy. By the end of the book, cases will be closed, but the lives of the Rocky Bluff P.D. will keep on. We'll be able to catch up though in the next series to come."
http://www.fictionforyou.com/ http://www.marilynmeredith.blogspot.com–**J.Kaye, Book Blog**

No Sanctuary

No Sanctuary

F. M. Meredith

Oak Tree Press   Taylorville, IL

Oak Tree Press

Oak Tree Press books may be purchased for educational, business or sales
promotional purposes. Contact Publisher for quantity discounts.

First Edition, January 2009

Cover by MickADesign.com

ISBN 978-1-892343-55-0

LCCN:2008938461

Acknowledgements

Billie Johnson, publisher and friend

My wonderful critique group and especially Shirley Hickman who listened to and critiqued **No Sanctuary** more than once.

Other Books in F.M. Meredith's

Rocky Bluff series...

Smell of Death

Fringe Benefits

Bad Tidings

Final Respects

Dedication

To the San Joaquin chapter of Sisters in Crime for all their support and the great speakers who gave me lots of story ideas.

To the members of the Public Safety Writers Association for being such good friends and willingly passing on information and great stories.

And always, to my love and husband of more years than I can remember, for always being there, toting the luggage and the books, driving me places, suffering through uncomfortable airplane rides, selling books, and best of all, loving me.

Chapter 1

"Oh, boy." Officer Stacey Wilbur keyed her radio and requested assistance, quickly describing the single vehicle accident in front of her.

Working the four-to-midnight shift, Stacey had been returning from a burglary call at a secluded ranch located far into the foothills that backed the community of Rocky Bluff. When she maneuvered her police unit around a sharp corner, she came upon the light green Toyota smashed into the trunk of a massive oak tree.

It was obvious the accident had happened recently. Though not a busy road, there were enough homes and ranches nestled in the valleys for someone to have come upon the scene if it occurred much before her arrival.

Hoping for survivors, Stacey shined her flashlight beam in the open driver's window. Squashed against the bent steering wheel was the woman driver. Blood splattered the sea foam green seat and the floor of the car. The puddling blood hadn't congealed. The speedometer needle pointed to 75. Steam erupted from the radiator.

An abundance of dark hair, wet with blood, covered the victim's face. Though Stacey knew there wouldn't be any, she reached through the window to feel for a pulse on the women's neck. Nothing.

Stacey put her hand on the hood of the car. As she'd expected it was warm. Quickly, she went over a check-list in her mind. There were no witnesses to question. The driver was dead. There was not enough traffic on the country road at that hour to worry about.

Despite the unrelenting Santa Ana winds that had been blowing down the canyons for the last two days, there didn't seem to be any danger of fire. Usually ocean breezes kept the southern California beach town cool, but they didn't have a chance against the power of the seasonal blast coming from the deserts.

Going back to her unit, Stacey called in the license number on the plates. While she waited for the information, she suspected this was more than an accident.

Using her cell phone, she dialed Doug Milligan's home number. A homicide detective, he was also a special friend of Stacey's. If they could find a way to spend more time together, their relationship might develop into more than a friendship. She often reflected on how wonderful it felt the few times she had been in his arms.

She should call the duty sergeant, but she could do that after she talked to Doug.

He answered on the first ring. "Milligan."

"Hi, it's Stacey."

His voice immediately softened. "Aren't you working tonight?"

"Yes, that's why I'm calling you. I'm at the scene of an accident, but it looks like it might be more than that."

"Tell me where you are and what you've found."

She gave him a quick description, ending with,

"...there's blood on the seat of the car and the floor."

He interrupted. "Do you know who it is?"

"No, I can't see her face and I haven't touched anything except when I tried for a pulse."

"I'll be there in a few minutes," Doug said.

"Do you want me to call the sergeant?"

"Who's on tonight?"

"Abel Navarro."

"No, I'll do it. Don't let anyone touch anything."

Stacey heard the approaching wail of sirens.

* * *

Doug dressed quickly. It never failed. No sooner had he put his head down on the pillow when the phone rang summoning him to a suspicious death. No one ever seemed to die under questionable circumstances in the day time. Rather than an annoyance, the call charged his adrenalin—and since it came from Stacey, he was eager to go.

A vision of her came into his mind, bringing a smile to his lips. Though he'd known Stacey since she'd started on the Rocky Bluff Police Department, he hadn't become attracted to her until she'd helped him solve three murder cases. He'd always admired her ability to defuse tense situations and to talk the toughest suspects into handcuffs. When he'd expressed his admiration, she'd shrugged off the praise with, "Hey, I know that almost everyone I come up against will be bigger than me, that's why I have to out-think them."

As he noticed how her short, gleaming honey-colored hair curled around her ears and at the back of her slim neck, and how her deceiving femininity and vulnerability contrasted with her internal toughness, it wasn't long before his admiration turned into something more. Though not glamorous like Doug's former wife, Stacey had wonderful characteristics Kerrie lacked.

Stacey loved law enforcement almost as much as he did.

Unfortunately they worked different shifts, and coupled with Stacey's devotion to her five-year-old son, they hadn't had much time to develop a relationship, even though the he knew the attraction was mutual. He had to take some of the blame; his dating skills were pretty rusty. Since his divorce, his job had taken up the major part of his life, and if he were being honest, before the divorce too.

Doug wet-combed his thick dark hair, strapped on his shoulder holster, fastened his badge to his belt, and hurried down the uncarpeted stairs of his Victorian home trying not to clatter and wake his renter, fellow police officer, Gordon Butler.

Using his cell, Doug called Navarro. Newly promoted to sergeant, Abel didn't seem disturbed that Stacey by-passed him to report the suspected homicide to Doug.

Abel's response was a quick, "I'll meet you out there."

Doug stashed the cell and started his vintage MG.

* * *

Stacey had done a good job securing the scene. She had crime tape surrounding a large area. Far enough away not to cover any skid marks or other evidence, a fire truck was parked, its personnel leaning against it.

Hurrying toward Doug, the wind whipped Stacey's hair and snatched at her uniform. "The ambulance has been and gone. No one has touched anything. The victim was an obvious code blue. I told the firemen they could leave too, but they're worried this wind might kick up a spark."

"Did you find out who the car belongs to?"

"Yes, I called it in. The vic may be someone I sort

of know. The car is registered to Reverend Paul Cookmeyer and his wife Mallory. I think the victim is Mrs. Cookmeyer. I can't be sure because I haven't see her face, but the hair is the right color and the build right."

Doug frowned, the name was familiar, but he couldn't place it. There were lots of churches in Rocky Bluff and he didn't attend any of them, not that he had anything against formal religion, there just wasn't enough time to squeeze anything else in.

"Tell me what you know about the Cookmeyers," he said, walking toward the driver's door of the Toyota. The left front fender was embedded into the unyielding trunk of the oak.

"He's the minister of Rocky Bluff Community Church." Stacey hurried along beside him. "That's the church my folks and little boy attend. Me too when I get a chance, which isn't often, I'm afraid."

"The big church on the bluff." Doug bent over and shined his pen light inside the car. As Stacey had described, blood splattered the seat and the floor.

A police unit drove up and braked to a squeaking stop on the other side of the fire truck. Without looking, Doug knew it was Abel.

Moving his flashlight beam back and forth, Doug searched in vain for footprints or anything else suspicious. It hadn't rained all summer so the ground was hard and dry. Golden brown, the weeds and grass crunched underfoot. Explosive chaparral covered the hillsides. No wonder the firemen waited.

Again, Doug peered inside the window at the victim. Blood matted dark hair that hid the face. The slim body was clothed in a light-weight beige jacket of expensive material, matching skirt hiked up to reveal tan legs and feet in high-heeled sandals.

"What've you got so far?" Abel approached Doug. "Hi, Stacey."

She nodded.

"It didn't happen long ago. The engine is warm.

The body isn't in rigor. Stacey, tell him who you think it is," Doug said.

When she did, Abel lifted his straight black eyebrows and frowned. "Tough break. I've notified the coroner's office, are you ready for them?"

"Sure."

Abel asked," What's the story here?"

"Looks like an accident, but won't know for sure until the coroner takes a look at the body."

"I didn't spot any skid marks," Abel said.

Doug nodded. "Me either. While we're waiting for the coroner, lets get some photos and see what else we can learn." Doug flipped open his notebook and began jotting notes.

Abel went back to his unit for a camera.

By the time the coroner's van arrived, photographs of the vehicle had been taken from every angle possible, along with what shots they could get of the victim without touching anything. Fingerprints had been collected from all logical outside surfaces of the Toyota, and some that weren't so logical, and attached to cards with the locations noted.

Stacey and Doug had combed the general area searching for anything that might be classified as evidence. The rearview mirror was set for a woman the size of the victim. The only substantial item was a snake skin purse on the floor of the front seat. That too would be collected by the coroner and taken to his office, to be turned over to the detectives later.

"The lady seems to have expensive clothes for a preacher's wife," Doug noted.

"Reverend Cookmeyer is no ordinary preacher," Stacey said.

"Why do you say that?"

"Because the Rocky Bluff Community Church brings in a lot of money, Cookmeyer has a substantial salary. He and his wife always wear the latest fashions. The church members are proud of the way they look."

Before she could continue, Eliseo Alvarado, a

deputy coroner, arrived. "More than a traffic accident, you think?" A tiny gnome-like fellow with olive skin, and long, thin black hair, he was known for his gallows humor.

"Possibly. Waiting for your opinion, of course." Doug pointed to the body.

All three of the police officers watched as the coroner slipped on latex gloves and began his work. When he brushed the blood-matted hair away from the victim's face, he said, "Oh, ho, what do we have here?" He'd exposed a small wound to her right temple with visible tattooing. "The victim was shot at close range with a small caliber gun."

"I thought it might be something like that." Doug shifted his weight, and scribbled in his notebook.

Before the coroner's deputy and his assistant took the body away, the coroner retrieved the woman's purse. Inside the wallet was her driver's license with her photograph and name. Mallory Cookmeyer.

"Let's notify the husband and find out if he knew where his wife was going this evening," Doug said. Sometimes the coroner made the death notification, at others it was the police department.

"Fine with me."

Doug glanced at Stacey. "You up to it?"

Stacey made a face. "I had a feeling you were going to give me the job."

"If you really don't want to..."

She touched his chest. "No, of course I'll do it."

"You'll need to find out if he knows where his wife was supposed to be. What her plans for the evening were. And pay close attention to his reaction to the news. Learn whatever else you can, and let him know that we'll want to talk to him tomorrow.

"Abel and I will finish here. I'll be at the station when you're done."

* * *

Stacey knew it was important for her to find out as much as possible from Reverend Cookmeyer. Whenever a woman was murdered, the husband and/or boyfriend became the first suspect. But she couldn't imagine Cookmeyer being a murderer, after all he was a man of the cloth. She laughed to herself. It wouldn't be the first time a preacher broke the law—man's or God's. Still, it didn't seem likely.

She'd talk to her folks and find out what they knew about Cookmeyer, his marriage, and his past.

The well-lit, flag-stone path curved its way through the lush green lawn toward the brick terrace leading to the white double-doors of the Cookmeyers' large Cape Cod style home located on the bluffs and about three-blocks from their church. Stacey didn't know if the luxurious home actually belonged to the Cookmeyers or was owned by the church. That was something else she'd have to ask her parents.

She pressed the doorbell and heard the sound of chimes echoing inside. She waited a few minutes before setting them ringing again. It was at least five more minutes before she heard movement on the other side of the door. Finally, it opened slowly.

Cookmeyer, though merely in his early forties, had a thick shock of white hair which at the moment was disarrayed. His tall, lean body was wrapped in a dark blue terry robe with a gold crest. He had on navy-and-white striped silk pajamas, and his feet were bare. It appeared Stacey had awakened him.

He blinked his blue eyes at her, a puzzled expression on his un-lined deeply tanned face. "Yes? Don't I know you?"

"Yes, sir. I'm Officer Wilbur. I come to your church sometimes, and my folks Clara and Clyde Osborne are members."

He smiled broadly, and extended his hand. "Yes, yes, of course. Stacey, isn't it?"

She was surprised he remembered her name. The church had three Sunday morning services because of its large membership. "Yes, sir."

The smile disappeared. "What is it? Why are you here? You have some bad news?"

"Yes, sir. I'm afraid I do. May I come in?"

He opened the door wider. "Certainly." He led the way through a tiled entry filled with plants, into a darkened living room. He switched on a lamp, revealing a spacious area furnished with an intriguing mix of antiques and modern furniture, the overall color scheme a blend of pale greens, yellows and off-white. "Have a seat, please." He pointed to a large, overstuffed circular couch that faced the white marble fireplace.

He absently backed toward a nearby wing-back chair. "This isn't about Mallory, is it?"

"I'm afraid so, sir."

But before she could say anything more, he said, "Where is she? Is she okay?"

There was no gentle way to deliver the news." No, sir, I'm sorry to have to tell you, but your wife Mallory is dead."

"Dead? Was she in an accident?" He took another step backwards as though he'd received a physical blow and sank into the chair. "How? What happened?"

"There was an accident, but I'm afraid there's more to it than that."

"I don't understand. What do you mean, more to it?" He blinked his eyes several times and his forehead furrowed. His reaction wasn't unusual. It often took awhile for such bad news to sink in.

"There's reason to believe your wife was murdered."

"Murdered? I don't understand."

"Mrs. Cookmeyer was shot."

Cookmeyer blinked and his mouth dropped open. "Oh, my dear God. Who would do such a thing?"

"Sir, we don't know yet. Perhaps you can help us. Did you know your wife's plans for this evening?"

He shook his head, running his fingers through his thick mane. "I can't think. I'm sure she must have mentioned it, but I left the house before seven. I went to the church to practice my sermon, and she was still home."

"Maybe it will come to you later. Detective Milligan will want to talk to you tomorrow. Perhaps you'll remember by then. Sir, is there someone I can call for you? You should have someone here with you."

Tears flooded his eyes. "Mallory, gone, I can't believe it." He shook his head again. "Isn't it funny, I've often had the role of the consoler. Now that I'm on the other end, I can't even think what I should do."

"Is there a family member or a friend who is particularly close to you? Someone who can come over and stay? Give you a hand?"

"What will I do about church tomorrow? I can't possibly preach a sermon."

"That's why you need someone to help you solve these problems. Who can I call?"

He stood and began pacing the floor. "Mallory's dead...murdered that's all I can think about."

Stacey got to her feet. "I know how hard this is. What about your secretary? Wouldn't she know who to get in touch with?"

He halted. "Oh, good idea. Katherine will know what to do."

"What's her number?"

"Oh, dear, I can't think."

"Tell me her name, I'll ask information."

"It's Katherine Danfelt. Her number is the first one on the list by the phone in the kitchen."

Everything was spotless in the house. The kitchen was ivory with splashes of blue and green. She found the phone on the tile counter, a memo pad with names and numbers beside it. Despite the lateness of the hour, the call was answered on the first ring.

"Ms. Danfelt, this is Officer Wilbur of the Rocky Bluff Police Department, and I'm afraid I have some bad news."

"Oh, dear, what is it?"

"Mrs. Cookmeyer has been murdered."

But before Stacey could say more, the secretary gasped, and blurted, "Oh, no, the reverend killed his wife."

Chapter 2

By the time Stacey returned to the police station, it was nearly two a.m. She found Doug in his small office, at his desk and using his computer.

After relating everything that had happened, Stacey finished with the secretary's strange reaction. "Someone needs to question her and find out why she thought Cookmeyer murdered his wife."

Doug scribbled on a pad. "One of a long list of things to do tomorrow. What happened next?"

"She immediately regretted what she said. Told me to forget it, didn't know what had got into her, and so on. Asked what she could do. I told her that her boss needed help. She said, 'Of course', and she turned up in about fifteen minutes. Taking control, she started making phone calls. After a bit, I was able to leave."

"What do you think? Could this guy be the killer?"

Stacey shrugged. "I don't know. His reactions to

the news about his wife seemed pretty normal. He guessed right away I'd come to see him about her."

"Maybe it wasn't a guess, maybe he knew because he killed her."

"If that were so, surely he would have acted differently."

"Could be he's really crafty and maybe it was kind of a reverse psychology thing."

"When I told him what happened, he didn't believe me at first. He didn't break down, but he seemed genuinely sad and shaken."

"He's probably seen all kinds of folks react to bad news. He knew exactly how to act. Something to consider anyway." Doug jotted a few notes before glancing at her again. "You better go home and get some sleep."

"What about you?"

"Got a few more things I need to get done. I've got to fill Frank in on what's going on." Frank Marshall was the other homicide detective. When Frank's partner of many years retired, Doug was appointed in his place.

"We'll have to decide exactly what we're going to give to the public and turn it over to Strickland."

Ryan Strickland, an officer who'd always sought publicity, had recently been made Public Information Officer. "Since the Reverend Cookmeyer has such a prominent position in the community, once the news gets out about his wife's murder, the media will bombard us."

Stacey backed toward the door. "Okay. I'll write my report and get it to you sometime tomorrow." She added, "I mean today."

"No big hurry." He turned to face her. "One of these days we've got to get together again. I haven't seen Davey for ages."

"He's been asking about you." Stacey smiled. "I keep telling him how busy you are." Waving, she left the room.

* * *

Abel Navarro slipped into bed and snuggled up to his wife's back. He kissed her ear.

"Ummm," Maria murmured and turned over to face him. "Did my own sweet sergeant have a good evening?"

"Exciting one. We had a murder. You may have heard of the victim, Mallory Cookmeyer?"

Maria opened her big, large eyes. "Name sounds kind of familiar but can't place her."

"Wife of the preacher of that big church on the bluffs."

"Oh, sure. Seen her picture on TV and in the paper. She does a lot of charity work."

"Not anymore, she doesn't."

"Who killed her?"

"Don't know yet, but whoever it was tried to make it look like an accident."

Maria frowned. "Was there much blood?"

"Plenty."

Maria's frown deepened. "Were you wearing a mask and the goggles I gave you?" She was a nurse at the local hospital.

"No, Maria. But it's okay, I didn't touch anything."

"Abel, Abel, Abel. You don't realize how dangerous blood can be."

"Honey, I got the Hepatitis shots like you told me."

"There isn't a vaccine for AIDS."

"You've told me."

"We don't really know if blood particles stay suspended in the air."

"The way the wind is blowing, I don't think that was a problem."

"Good."

"What about your hands? Did you wash them thoroughly?"

"Yes, Maria. I even took a shower before I got into bed."

She giggled. "Then what are you waiting for?" She grabbed his behind and pulled him closer; her lips poised for a kiss.

* * *

"You were out late. Something happen last night?" Gordon asked. He sat at the round dining room table, a cup of coffee near his elbow, a thick book open in front of him.

Despite only three hours sleep, Doug was anxious to get to the station. "Any coffee left?"

"Just made a full pot. Still some scrambled eggs in the pan."

"Great." Doug poured himself a cup and scooped the eggs out onto a plate. "A woman got murdered last night." He sat down across from Gordon, and began eating.

"Oh, yeah? Who?"

"A Mrs. Mallory Cookmeyer. Her husband is some kind of celebrity preacher."

"I've heard of him. White-haired, good-looking guy. Lots of charm. I gave him a ticket once."

Doug grinned. "You've given everyone in this town a ticket."

"Not everyone," Gordon said.

"What're you doing?"

"Studying the laws."

"What for? You know them better than anyone in the department."

"Hey, never hurts to be prepared."

"You ought to try giving someone some slack once in awhile."

Two red circles appeared on Gordon's already pink cheeks. "My job is to enforce the law."

Gordon's wife left him for another police officer who killed his first wife and nearly got away with it. Since that time, Gordon had become over-zealous in his efforts to be the perfect law enforcement officer because of his perceived failure as a husband.

Doug sipped his coffee and tried not to make a face. One thing Gordon didn't know how to do was make coffee.

"Identified the killer?" Gordon asked.

"Not yet."

"Got any ideas?"

"The husband is always the first suspect, but it's much too soon to even speculate about that." Against his better judgment, Doug took another big swig of the black, foul tasting liquid. If nothing else, it should pack enough caffeine in his system to keep him going for awhile.

Doug emptied the cup, grabbed his suit jacket but didn't put it on. When he stepped outside, it was like walking into a blast furnace. Weren't the Santa Ana winds ever going to quit?

* * *

"You should have called me last night." His words were scolding but the tone was not, as Frank Marshall leaned back in his chair and polished his bald pate with his palm.

"It was late and Officer Wilbur and Sergeant Navarro gave me a hand."

Marshall winked. "So how's it going with you and Wilbur?"

"It's at a standstill. We never seem to have the same days off, and she's working the p.m. shift right now."

"You better get a move on, pal. Stacey's a great catch and she needs a daddy for her little boy. She isn't going to wait forever for you to get off your duff."

"Thanks, Frank. Makes me feel a whole lot better."

Marshall grinned. "Don't want to see you left out in the cold. Now, tell me what we've got on this murder and where we need to go with the investigation." He reached in his pocket and pulled out a pack of gum. Once a heavy smoker, now he chewed gum.

After Doug filled Marshall in with what Stacey had told him about Reverend Cookmeyer, he finished with, "She felt he reacted appropriately to the news about his wife."

"Uh-huh, but you've got to remember, most preachers are actors at heart. They get up in front of their congregations at least once a week to emote and posture like any other performer."

"I hadn't thought about that, but I do know because of his profession he's seen plenty of examples of how people respond to bad news about their loved ones."

"Uh huh." Marshall printed the word HUSBAND in caps at the top of a yellow legal pad and began doodling hangmen's nooses around it. "Has he got an alibi?"

"I don't think Stacey got that specific with him."

"We'll have to do that sometime soon."

"There's something else. When Stacey told Cookmeyer's secretary about the murder, the woman's immediate response was that he'd killed his wife."

Marshall printed SECRETARY under HUSBAND. "Got a name for her?"

Doug flipped through a couple of pages in his own notebook. "Yep. Katherine Danfelt."

"Get hold of her right away and set up an appointment. Make one with Cookmeyer too." He leaned forward in his chair. "Before we go off half-cocked, you're sure this isn't a drive-by shooting?"

"Oh, yeah. Mrs. Cookmeyer was shot in the right temple. The passenger window was closed and intact."

"Okay. Sounds to me if all goes well, we could

have our murderer in jail by this evening."

Doug hoped it would be that way, but his gut instinct was that it was going to be more complicated than that.

* * *

By the time Stacey got up, her parents were finishing breakfast and Davey was in the living room watching cartoons on the TV.

"How was your night, dear?" Clara asked as she cleared the table. Everything about her was round and soft. Her bobbed salt-and-pepper hair curled around her smiling face. She took in Stacey's tailored blouse and pants suit. "Are you planning on going to church with us this morning?"

"Thought I would." Stacey kissed her father on the forehead as he started to rise. "There's something I need to tell both of you."

Clara turned expectantly, a hint of smile on her lips.

"Maybe you should sit down, Mom." Stacey poured herself a cup of coffee.

Pulling out a chair, Clara settled into it. "What is it? Not bad news, I hope."

Leaning against the sink, Stacey nodded. "I'm afraid so. Mallory Cookmeyer was killed last night."

Clara's hand flew to her open mouth. "Oh."

Her husband of nearly forty years frowned and his bushy gray brows nearly came together as the line bisecting his forehead deepened. His steel gray hair was cut in the same short military style he'd worn nearly his whole life. "Are you sure, honey?"

After sipping her coffee, Stacey said, "Oh, yes, Dad, I'm positive. I saw her."

"Poor, poor Reverend Cookmeyer." Clara brushed a tear from her eye.

"What was it? Drunk driver or something?" Clyde asked.

"At first it appeared to be an accident. However, once the coroner got there, we learned that Mrs. Cookmeyer had been shot." She watched her parents' reaction. Disbelief widened Clara's eyes, and Clyde's mouth dropped open.

"Why would anyone want to kill Mallory Cookmeyer?" her father asked.

"We don't know yet. You have any ideas?"

"Goodness no," Clara said. "Mallory is...was...a lovely young woman." A shadow crossed her plump, pleasant face.

Stacey knew she'd thought of something. "What is it, Mom?"

"Nothing, really, merely some gossip I heard, but it couldn't possibly have any bearing on Mallory's...uh...death." Murder wasn't a word Clara could use easily.

"Tell me what you were thinking, okay?"

Clara shook her head. "You know how I feel about gossip."

"Yes, Mom. Unless it's something that could help solve the case, it won't go any further."

"You know your father and I have been members of Rocky Bluff Community Church ever since it met in that tiny white building downtown."

Stacey had only attended the church at that location a couple of times. She remembered it as having only a handful of people seated in the folding chairs.

Her father chimed in. "It wasn't until Paul Cookmeyer became the minister that it started to grow."

"Where did he come from?"

"He'd been a Presbyterian minister down south, but he broke away from them for some reason I can't remember. Our former minister died, and Paul answered an ad we'd run in the 'L.A. Times'."

While he spoke, Clara refilled her husband's coffee cup. "More, dear?" She gestured toward Stacey with the pot, seeming relieved that Clyde had taken over.

"Sure. Go on, Dad."

"When he came to us, we only had thirty members and on a good day, maybe fifteen attended. It wasn't long before word got around town about Cookmeyer's dynamic preaching and our congregation swelled."

"Don't forget all the things he's done for the community," Clara prompted.

"Let's see, there's the lunch program for the homeless and the poor. Wasn't he instrumental in starting the women's shelter?"

Clara sat back down next to Clyde. "Oh, yes. Back then Mallory was right beside him doing all the things preachers' wives usually do."

"Which means she changed?"

"That's what I was going to tell you," Clara said. "She was so young and enthusiastic when they first began with our church."

"But of course she got older and I suppose she lost her enthusiasm. Have any idea why?" Stacey asked.

"I only know what I've heard."

"Which is what?" Stacey fought to keep the impatience out of her voice.

"Others took over. Lots of women are attracted by Reverend Cookmeyer's good looks and, Clyde, what's that other word everyone uses to describe him?"

"Charisma."

"Yes, that's it, charisma. He certainly has plenty of that. He always has lots of female volunteers for everything, and my guess is that Mallory no longer felt needed."

Davey laughed loudly at something on the television causing Stacey to think of another question. "What about children?"

"Once she confided in me that she couldn't have any. I suppose it's all right to tell you since she isn't here anymore. Oh my goodness, I just can't believe it." Clara's eyes filled with tears and one slid down her lightly rouged cheek.

"Tell me what, Mom?"

"She wanted to adopt a child, but her husband, Reverend Cookmeyer, didn't. He told her they could fill their need by helping the children in the church. As time went by she seemed less and less concerned about church events. Don't get me wrong, she always made an appearance, but she no longer headed any committees or even acted very interested in what was going on."

"Yep, showed up and looked pretty, that was about it. Frankly, I don't think he paid enough attention to her." Clyde shot his suit jacket sleeve and glanced at his watch. "If you've got any more questions, they're going to have to wait. If we don't get moving we aren't going to make it to the last service this morning. We've already missed Sunday School."

"Let me grab my purse." Though Stacey knew she couldn't talk to anyone until after the church service, and perhaps not even then, it would be interesting and maybe even informative to note people's reactions to the news about their preacher's wife.

* * *

"Hated to tear you away from your family on a Sunday," Doug said. "But figured you'd want in on this from the beginning. Going to be a big one as far as the media is concerned."

Doug met Ryan Strickland in the hall outside his office, while Frank remained inside making phone calls.

"You did the right thing," Strickland said, flashing his mouthful of perfect, bright teeth. "To be honest, going to Mass every Sunday isn't my favorite pastime though Barbara wouldn't miss it for the world. Must have a darn good excuse to satisfy her. Fortunately police work is about the only acceptable one."

Barbara Strickland had once been married to Doug's best friend who was killed in the line of duty.

Though Doug had been surprised that Barbara married so soon after her husband's death, he was even more surprised by her choice. A true publicity-hound, Strickland had never seemed like a candidate for the position of "family-man". But so far, Strickland seemed to be pleased with his new role, though Doug suspected that it was mostly because outsiders thought him quite a hero for marrying the bereaved widow and taking on the responsibility of being a step-father to her three sons.

"How are Barbara and the boys? Haven't seen them for awhile," Doug asked.

"Barbara's trying hard to make me fat." Strickland patted his flat stomach. "She's such a good cook, that I've had to double my workouts. You'll have to come over for dinner one night and you can see the boys for yourself. Growing like weeds, of course, into Scouts and every sport there is. They keep us hopping."

Doug felt a sharp twinge of jealousy. Strickland was enjoying all the fruits of fatherhood while Doug seldom saw his own children, thanks to Kerrie, his ex, remarrying and moving to San Diego, taking the kids with her.

"Now that I'm here, tell me what's going on so I'll know how to handle things." Strickland sat military straight, his clean-shaven face exhibiting curiosity as he flipped open a tablet.

Quickly filling him in on what little he knew so far, Doug ended with, "I'm heading over to give Reverend Cookmeyer my condolences as soon as we're finished here."

"I've bumped into the deceased a time or two, a real looker. The press will have a field day with this one. How about if I tag along? Maybe I can give you a hand."

Doug shrugged. "Why not?" He wasn't sure whether Strickland wanted to be helpful or just needed an excuse to be away from his ready-made family and their event-packed Sunday schedule.

While sliding his arm into the sleeve of his jacket, Frank strode through the door. "Hey, Strickland. Let's get a move on, Cookmeyer is expecting us."

"I'll follow you in my car, in case something comes up," Strickland said.

* * *

Word about Mallory's death spread quickly. The congregation was already buzzing before the assistant minister made the announcement. Stacey was pleased that he kept it simple and didn't mention anything about murder.

Almost immediately she heard a loud whisper from a woman sitting behind her that piqued her interest.

"H'mmm. Should make Sally Jo happy."

Another voice answered, "Wonder how long it will take before Paul and Sally Jo let those who haven't already guessed know how they feel about each other?"

Loud chords from the organ drowned out any further comment that might have come from the gossips. Stacey resisted an urge to turn around and ask some questions of her own. Instead she studied the choir director's straight, long hair and waving arms, as Sally Jo Roberts led the huge choir in a resounding hymn. Stacey wondered if it were true. Was there really something going on between the petite Sally Jo and the Reverend Cookmeyer? Another tidbit to pass on to Doug and to ask her parents about.

* * *

The detectives and Strickland gathered on the porch of Cookmeyers' home. "Classy digs." Strickland said while surveying the surroundings. "Had no idea preachers lived like this. The priests at St. Mark's are housed in that old brick place next to the church."

Doug pressed the doorbell and chimes resounded inside.

"Hey, what about those TV ministers. Bet they don't do so bad for themselves." Marshall stuck a fresh stick of gum in his mouth.

"Yeah, I know. But after all Rocky Bluff isn't all that big and there's lots of churches around."

"But Cookmeyer's has way more members than any of the rest," Doug said, just as the front door opened.

A woman in her late forties or early fifties opened the door. Her extremely short hair was dyed black, her heavy make-up didn't hide the sagging lids and the bags beneath her large dark eyes that narrowed as she studied each of the men. Silver-framed glasses hung on a chain against her ample bosom. Plump everywhere, she wore a black pants suit with a long jacket, and a black-and-white polka dotted blouse. "Yes?" she said, barely moving her full, bright red lips.

"We're hear to see Reverend Cookmeyer," Marshall announced, flipping his wallet to expose his badge and identification. "Detective Frank Marshall, and this is Detective Milligan, and Public Information Officer Strickland."

She tipped her head and frowned at Strickland's title. "What does that mean, Public Information Officer?"

"Excuse me, ma'am, but we're here to see the preacher," Marshall said, a bit testily.

The woman crossed her arms, shifted her weight until her feet were slightly apart and glared at Marshall. "I'm Reverend Cookmeyer's private secretary, Mrs. Danfelt."

Dressed in a dark gray pin-striped suit, his white hair swept back from his wide forehead, Paul Cookmeyer appeared behind Mrs. Danfelt and put a hand on her shoulder. "It's all right, Katherine."

Mrs. Danfelt didn't budge. "You don't need a bunch of gossiping..."

"Step aside, Katherine, let the gentlemen in."

Still glowering, the secretary moved beside a huge Boston fern in a gleaming brass pot.

The officers followed the preacher into his elegant living room. "Please, sit down. Perhaps you'd like some coffee?"

"Not right now, thanks." Marshall settled himself on one end of the crescent-shaped couch.

Doug sat in the middle and Strickland at the far end, while Cookmeyer chose a big wing chair across from them.

With her red lips pursed, and her arms still crossed over her bosom, Katherine Danfelt perched on the edge of a Victorian-style chair.

"We'd like to begin by offering our condolences for your loss," Marshall said, as he pulled his notebook from his suit jacket.

Cookmeyer nodded, a sad smile on his narrow lips. "It's still hard to believe."

"You'll need to go to the coroner's office in Ventura sometime today to make an official identification of the body," Doug said.

"On Sunday?" Katherine sounded incredulous. "Why couldn't I do that?"

Doug smiled at the woman. He had a feeling that somehow they needed to get on her good side. As Cookmeyer's secretary, she could be a key to the case. "Nice of you to offer, ma'am, but it needs to be a member of the family. It should be done as quickly as possible. When we're through here, one of us would be glad to take you."

Again Cookmeyer nodded, but Doug's efforts had little effect on the secretary who mumbled something about "inconsiderate oafs."

"Have you any idea what your wife's plans were for yesterday evening?"

Cookmeyer rubbed his temple with two fingers. "You know, I've wracked my brain, and I truly can't remember. She did say something about having to go out, but I don't know if she mentioned where. I must admit, I probably was focused on something else."

"Would you mind telling us exactly where you were from, say around seven and the time Officer Wilbur brought you the news of your wife's demise?" Marshall held his pen poised above his open notebook.

"Like I told the young woman, I was over at the church practicing my sermon. I'm not sure what time I got home...around nine-thirty or ten perhaps. I listened to some music and read awhile, took a shower and went to bed."

"Did anyone see you at the church?" Doug asked.

Cookmeyer shrugged. "Let's see, when I first arrived I popped in to say 'hi' to the youth group having a get-together in fellowship hall. The leaders and all the kids saw me."

"What about later?" Doug prompted.

"No, afraid not. I practiced my sermon in the sanctuary as I do most Saturday evenings. No one else was there."

"What about Sally Jo?" Mrs. Danfelt asked. "Don't you usually arrive about the time she finishes choir practice?"

Cookmeyer's white eyebrows gathered together as he frowned at her. "No, no. I didn't see Sally Jo."

"Are you sure?" Mrs. Danfelt persisted.

"Of course I'm sure," Cookmeyer snapped.

"Excuse me," Doug asked, "Who is Sally Jo?"

Before the minister could answer, the doorbell rang. Mrs. Danfelt jumped to her feet. "What now?"

Chapter 3

A heavy-set man with thinning dark hair, rushed toward Cookmeyer. "I heard the news from one of my congregation and rushed right over. My word, Paul, this is dreadful. Poor Mallory. How are you holding up?" He clasped the taller Cookmeyer in a bear hug.

Upon releasing him, the new arrival noticed the other occupants of the room. "Oh, I'm sorry, I've interrupted something here." He rubbed his palms together before extending a hand toward Frank Marshall. "I'm Jared Love, pastor of All Saint's Calvary, and a good friend of the Cookmeyers."

From behind Pastor Love, Mrs. Danfelt made a rude sounding noise. Doug wondered what that was all about.

All Saint's Calvary Church was a huge brick edifice located in the downtown area, but that was the only thing Doug knew about it.

Marshall flipped open his wallet to display his

identification and badge while he introduced himself and Doug.

Pastor Love wrinkled his brow, glancing at Cookmeyer. "Is there something I can do for you, Paul?"

"When I'm free, I'd like to talk to you about the funeral," Cookmeyer said.

"Of course, anything." He took a few steps backwards. "Obviously this isn't a good time. Why don't you give me a call later today?"

"I'll do that," Cookmeyer said.

Before Pastor Love reached the door, Mrs. Danfelt muttered, "Good riddance."

"Katherine, for goodness sake," Cookmeyer scolded.

She glared toward the entrance hall. "I don't trust that man and you shouldn't either."

Addressing the police officers, Cookmeyer said, "As you can see, my secretary has definite opinions about everything.

* * *

The phone rang as soon as Stacey and her family stepped inside the home she and her son shared with her parents. It was Doug asking her to interview Mrs. Danfelt.

As he'd suggested, she called the minister's home and learned Mrs. Danfelt was still there. Though Mrs. Danfelt sounded reluctant, she agreed to meet with Stacey.

In a few minutes she was once again in Reverend Cookmeyer's home, only this time she'd been taken to his kitchen and sat across the white table from his secretary, Katherine Danfelt.

"Since you attend our church, I suppose I can trust you." Mrs. Danfelt poured both of them a cup of coffee. "At least you seem to have more compassion than those buffoons that came earlier. How they can intrude upon a poor widower's grief like that, I don't understand."

"That's their job. They have to question everyone who might be a suspect in Mrs. Cookmeyer's death."

Mrs. Danfelt pursed her red lips. "Surely no one could possibly think Reverend Cookmeyer had anything to do with his wife's death."

"Have you forgotten? That's the first thing you said to me when you heard about it."

She shook her head. "I already told you I don't know why I said that. You startled me. It just popped out."

"Everyone who was close to Mrs. Cookmeyer must be questioned. It's merely a matter of finding out where people were at the time she was killed," Stacey said.

"As long as you're here, I might as well tell you others had reason to want something to happen to Mallory."

"I'll be glad to listen to anything you consider important."

Feeling discomfort because of Mrs. Danfelt's steady gaze, Stacey smiled as sweetly as possible at the other woman, hoping she conveyed a sympathetic attitude.

Finally, Mrs. Danfelt sighed loudly. "I suppose it's inevitable. What I have to say will come out eventually. But you must understand, my loyalties are with the Reverend. He is a wonderful man. Not perfect, mind you, but what man is? He's done so much for the community, I'd like to protect his reputation."

"Understandable." Stacey sipped her coffee and waited.

"I'm afraid Reverend Cookmeyer's marriage wasn't all that it could be. I don't have any way of knowing who was at fault, though I suppose it was him. He got too busy and didn't spend enough time with Mallory."

"Was there someone he did spend time with?"

Mrs. Danfelt swirled the dark liquid in her cup.

"I'm sure you are aware that women are attracted to Reverend Cookmeyer. He's always been extremely careful not to allow himself to be put into a bad position. He took great care to never be alone with any female member of the congregation. When he counseled one of the women, he insisted that I remain at my desk right outside his office. He always left the door ajar so he couldn't be accused of any wrongdoing."

"I notice that you're speaking in the past tense. Has something happened to change that?"

"I'm afraid so. I hate to even mention this, but I know you'll hear it soon enough from someone else. Of late, Reverend Cookmeyer has been very careless in his relationship with Sally Jo Roberts."

"The choir director?" Now it was getting interesting.

"He's the one who recommended her for the job of choir director."

"Which she does quite well."

"Oh, yes indeed. Of course she's extremely grateful to the Reverend, and they are close friends. I'm not sure when the friendship changed into something more, but I suspect it became serious about the same time he started closing the door when she came to visit him in his office. I warned him people might talk."

"You were right," Stacey said. "I heard something along those lines today in church."

"But it's important for you to understand that I'm sure Mallory didn't know, and if she did, she didn't care. In fact, I think Mallory might have been having an affair with someone herself."

That was something Stacey hadn't heard before. "Really? With who?"

"That's one of the things I wanted to tell you. Of course I don't have any real proof, but I just know that she has been seeing a lot of this man."

"Do you know his name?"

"Oh, I most certainly do. Jared Love. He even had the audacity to come to see Reverend Cookmeyer this morning."

The name sounded familiar. "Tell me something about him."

"He's the pastor of All Saint's Calvary Church. I can tell you, no matter what he might say, he's no fan of Reverend Cookmeyer."

"Why is that?"

"All Saint's was the biggest Protestant church in Rocky Bluff until Reverend Cookmeyer came along. Many of the members of All Saint's left to join Rocky Bluff Community. You know that didn't exactly make Pastor Love a fan."

The exodus of members wouldn't have endeared Love to Cookmeyer, so killing Mallory didn't seem logical. Especially if he was having an affair with her. "What makes you feel there was something between Mallory and Pastor Love?"

"She'd been seeing him on a regular basis. I think she was going to him for counseling about her marriage...though I don't really know for sure."

"How did you find out about this?"

"There were times she told me to tell Reverend Cookmeyer that's where she'd be. I think she did it to make him jealous." Mrs. Danfelt stood and brought a date book in a leather cover over to the table and slid it in front of Stacey. "Take a look at this."

It was opened to the week that immediately passed. Saturday afternoon Mallory had a hair appointment. Nine p.m. was circled but nothing written beside it.

* * *

Ryan Strickland arrived home to find his wife, Barbara, and the boys already there. Barbara was putting a large dish of lasagna on the table beside a huge bowl filled with salad. She grinned at him. "Hi, honey, you're just in time."

He slipped his arms around her waist and leaned down to kiss the top of her curly head. "You know I never miss one of your wonderful meals if I can help it."

"Oh, sweetheart. You're such a flatterer," she said.

"Mean every word of it. I'll go wash up."

"Holler at the boys too, will you? They're in their bedrooms changing."

He went down the hall towards the master bedroom he shared with Barbara. It completely amazed him how he'd settled into married life. Though he'd married Barbara primarily because it seemed to be a smart career move, she had completely won him over.

Though Barbara wasn't what he'd ever considered his type, he admired the great strength she'd displayed when her husband was killed in the line of duty. To be honest, taking care of her and her sons helped relieve the guilt he felt because he'd been the one who provided the gun to her husband's killer–though he'd never imagined what it would be used for. Of course no one knew his secret and it was something he wished he could forget.

It didn't take long for him to thoroughly enjoy the fact that Barbara couldn't do enough to make his life more comfortable. The biggest surprise was her enthusiasm in the bedroom, unexpected but joyfully accepted.

An odd thing had happened almost without his realizing it. When he'd first met Barbara he'd thought her plain and unattractive and a bit plump for his taste. But that opinion soon changed. Her fresh-scrubbed look now appealed to him far more than the overly made-up faces he once admired. Though she kept her body hidden beneath ordinary and sometimes baggy apparel, he knew that her skin had a glorious pink glow and felt like silk under his fingertips. Undressed, Barbara's figure seemed perfect. It certainly fit with his. He was delighted to know her many charms were reserved for him alone.

The boys sat around the table, impatiently waiting for him.

Once he seated himself at the head, the family made the sign of the cross, mumbled grace, and grabbed for the food.

"Honestly, you guys," Barbara scolded, "You act like you haven't eaten in a week."

"How was church?" Ryan asked.

The boys rolled their eyes but didn't stop shoveling in the food.

"It was very nice," Barbara said. "But I heard some sad news. That beautiful wife of the minister of the big church on the bluffs was killed. That's why you had to go to the station, isn't it?"

"Exactly. I'll be holding a press conference tomorrow."

"Oh, I'm glad I got your dark blue suit cleaned. I think you look terrific in it, distinguished even. Do you know who did it yet?" She frowned at her youngest son. "Philip, for goodness sake, chew your food."

"No, not yet. Of course, we're looking at the husband."

"I've seen him on T.V. Good looking fellow with that great white hair. Not as handsome as you, of course. Watch out, Daryl, don't reach across the table like that. Ask someone to pass what you want."

Barbara's incessant chatter used to drive Ryan crazy, but he no longer minded. Her good points far out-weighed her flaws. To be honest, he would have been happier if she could have totally concentrated on him. The boys took an awful lot of her time. She was almost the perfect wife but came even closer to being the perfect mother.

* * *

Stacey knew the primary reason for the dinner

invitation from Doug was so he could learn what she'd found out from Mrs. Danfelt, but she couldn't help the fact that her heart pounded with excitement at seeing him in a social setting. He'd kissed and hugged her in a friendly manner when he picked her up. After helping her into his MG, he grinned as he drove toward his favorite Chinese restaurant. "You look absolutely terrific."

She had dressed carefully, wearing a simple but elegant pink dress that clung to her slim figure, the flared skirt short enough to make her legs look longer.

He chatted about this and that, though she knew he was eager to hear about her interview with the Reverend Cookmeyer's secretary. But she also knew he wouldn't ask about what she'd learned until he could jot the significant information down.

Stacey had gone to the Chinese restaurant a couple of times with Doug and always wondered how he'd had nerve to eat there the first time. It was in a sleazy part of town, and the restaurant was situated over a Mexican bar. To reach the restaurant, they entered a weather-beaten door with peeling green paint and a dirty window that had Chinese writing painted on it. After climbing a narrow, poorly lighted flight of stairs, Doug pushed open the heavy door that led into the small establishment frequented mostly by Asian patrons.

The waitress seated them at a tiny booth and waited while Stacey glanced at the menu. The items listed were nothing like those in the Chinese restaurants she was used to. "What are you going to have?"

Doug suggested an entree with an odd sounding name.

Closing her menu, she smiled at the waitress and said, "I'll have that too."

Doug leaned across the table. "So tell me, how did it go?"

She quickly filled him in.

He scribbled in his notebook while she talked. When she'd finished, he asked, "So what do you think?

Is Cookmeyer having an affair with his choir director?"

"I don't know for sure, but people at church were buzzing about it. Even my mother, who never listens to that stuff, has heard the rumors."

They ate hot-and-sour soup while discussing what should happen next—at least her part in the investigation. She couldn't help but notice how blue Doug's eyes were, and how his dimples appeared even when he wasn't smiling.

"You don't mind do you?" he said, and she realized he had been speaking to her.

"I'm sorry, my thoughts were elsewhere." She could feel her cheeks warming.

"So I noticed. I wondered if I could get you to interview..." he glanced at his notepad beside his soup bowl, "Sally Jo Roberts for me. You're far better at finding out important details from women than I am."

"Sure, I'll be glad to. When do you want me to do it?" Actually she loved being in on a murder investigation. Not only was it fascinating, but it also gave her the opportunity to spend more time with Doug.

"Tomorrow morning, if you can." He wiped his mouth and patted his dark mustache with his napkin. "I'll make sure you get paid overtime."

"Thanks. I'll give Sally Jo a call first thing and set up an appointment. Now that Davey is in kindergarten, I have a little more time to myself." She smiled at the waitress who put a plate of rice, vegetables, mushrooms, and several plump shrimp in front of her. "Yum, this looks delicious."

"One of my favorites," Doug said. "Anything else I should know?"

"Mrs. Danfelt thinks Mallory might have been having an affair with Pastor Love. Supposedly she was being counseled by him."

Doug had a large forkful of food on the way to his mouth. He paused with it a few inches away. "Oh, really? I met Pastor Love this morning at the new widower's home. Cookmeyer asked Love to do Mallory's funeral."

He put the food in his mouth and chewed. "H'mmm. Love was sympathetic, but he didn't act like he'd lost someone he loved."

"I wonder if he's married," Stacey said.

Doug scribbled in the notebook.

"I don't think we should put too much weight on what Mrs. Danfelt had to say. By her own admission, she's willing to do anything to protect Cookmeyer's reputation."

Doug raised a dark eyebrow. "Even murder?"

"The thought crossed my mind. Mallory had nine o'clock p.m. circled on Saturday's page of her appointment book. Unfortunately, there wasn't anything written there to explain what she was planning to do then."

"Likely she had an appointment with someone who she didn't want her husband to know about. Maybe the person she was having an affair with. Or the person who murdered her."

"Could be the same one," Stacey said.

By the time they finished eating, Doug had filled her in completely on what he'd learned so far and what they needed to find out. For several minutes, they tossed around several theories about what might have happened.

He handed his credit card to the waitress when she brought the bill. To Stacey, he said, "Strickland will be making a press briefing in the morning. Once the news gets out we'll probably hear all sorts of interesting details about Mallory Cookmeyer and her husband."

When he opened the door at the bottom of stairs, a blast of hot wind struck them.

"Is this Santa Ana ever going to quit?" Stacey's skirt whipped around her thighs and she tried unsuccessfully to hold it down.

He grinned at her efforts. "Nice view. You've got great legs."

"Thanks."

"Do you have to go right home?"

She ought to of course, but if this relationship was ever going to go anywhere, she had to take advantage of whatever time they had together. "What did you have in mind?"

"Well, I thought we could go back to my place for dessert."

"What about Gordon?" It hadn't been too long ago since Gordon Butler had a crush on her.

"He's working this evening." Doug grinned. "I even baked a devil's food cake."

"My favorite.

"I remembered."

It was a short drive up the hill to Doug's restored Victorian. With his arm around her waist, he led her up the front walk and inside.

Stacey had eaten Doug's cooking before, he was as good a baker as a cook. Once they'd finished off huge pieces of the cake, they settled on the couch in the living room. Doug put his arm around her, his lips found hers, and Stacey returned his kiss. His lips were soft and felt wonderful against hers. The scent of his after-shave lotion was strong, his mouth tasted fresh and pepperminty. She felt herself melding against his strong body.

The front door banged open, interrupting the building passion. Gordon Butler's voice rang out, "Hey, Doug, you'll never guess what happened to me."

Chapter 4

"Oops, sorry, I didn't know you had company," Butler said. "Hi Stacey, how're you doing?"

Doug hoped Gordon would realize he'd interrupted something important and leave as suddenly as he'd appeared.

Stacey smiled at Doug and leaned around him to greet the intruder, smoothing her skirt as she did.

"You'll never guess what happened to me." He headed toward the oak table. "Wow, look at that cake. I'm going to get a piece."

"I'm sorry," Doug mouthed in Stacey's direction.

"It's okay. I really should be getting home," she said, though her sigh told him she was as disappointed as he.

Gordon was grinning like an idiot. "Don't you dare leave until I tell you what happened. It's absolutely unbelievable."

"Hey, Gordon, can't it wait until tomorrow? We were kind of in the middle of something here." Doug tightened his grip on Stacey's hand.

She squeezed back.

Gordon could have posed as an advertisement for the police department with his buff body filling out his navy blue uniform. His eyes flashed with excitement, his cheeks flushed, as he began his story. "You gotta hear this. The sergeant says I'm lucky to be alive."

"We might as well listen," Doug said, relaxing against the couch. He caressed Stacey's arm, and she settled against him.

"I pull this guy over for erratic driving. He starts hassling me as soon as I get him out of his vehicle. I take him around to the back and begin frisking him, when all of sudden this car comes out of the blue and runs into the back of my unit and sends it sailing toward me and the suspect. We both jump out of the way, but the suspect isn't fast enough and he gets hit. Broken leg, I think."

Butler chuckled. "Get this. The guy driving the other car gets out and comes charging at me, screaming, 'I meant to get you, you crazy, dumb cop.' Now this guy looks kind of familiar, but I can't really place him..."

"Come on, Gordon, can you get to the point?" Doug said.

Stacey smiled at Gordon. "It's okay, go ahead, tell us what happened."

Doug sighed and rolled his eyes.

"Hang on. This is a good one. Another unit pulls up and an ambulance arrives to take away the suspect. We haul the guy who ran into my car off to jail and guess who he turns out to be?" Gordon looked from one to the other, exposing his big, white teeth in an enormous grin.

"I have no idea," Doug said.

"Well, remember that guy I gave the parking ticket to who got so mad at me he filed a complaint?"

"There's been more than one of those since you decided to memorize the vehicle code and enforce it to the letter."

Undaunted, Gordon went on, "This was the guy that parked too far from the curb."

"Oh, I heard about that," Stacey said. "I was there when the man came into the department. What was he, eighteen and three-quarters of an inch away. You wrote him up for 3/4 of an inch."

"No wonder he was mad." Doug wished Gordon would evaporate.

"It would have been a lot easier if he'd just paid the ticket. Now he's been charged with attempted assault on a police officer, assault with a deadly weapon, and destruction of police property." Gordon puffed out his chest.

"Poor guy," Stacey whispered.

"That's quite a tale all right." Doug stood and helped Stacey to her feet. Still holding her hand, he led her toward the front door. "I'll be back in a while."

"No hurry, think I'll do some studying."

"Guy never knows when to quit," Doug mumbled.

Outside, he added, "I'm going to have to ask Gordon to move or I'll never have any privacy."

Stacey giggled." I know Gordon better than most. He can be pretty oblivious to what is going on around him, but he means well. You have to admit, that was a funny story."

* * *

Anxious to get to work on the Cookmeyer case, Doug arrived at the police station before seven a.m. The Santa Ana winds had finally subsided and the temperature cooled down to the mid-seventies. The phone rang as soon as he entered his office. He picked up the receiver in mid-ring. "Detective Milligan."

"Alvarado here. Got some interesting news for you about the Cookmeyer woman."

"What's that?" Doug sat behind his desk and pulled a notebook in front of him.

"No evidence of drugs or alcohol abuse. Gun shot killed her."

"So what's so interesting about that?"

"Keep your pants on, fellow. Your murder victim was pregnant."

"Okay. How far along?" Though intriguing, Doug wasn't sure how the news affected the case, or if it did.

"Around three months. I'll fax you the preliminary autopsy report sometime today. We'll release her belongings to the department whenever you want to come and get them. You going to let the preacher know he not only lost his wife but a child too?"

"Suppose I'll have to," Doug said, remembering what Stacey had told him about Mallory not being able to conceive.

Doug left a note for Frank, telling him where he was going and why. He headed for Cookmeyer's house. It was still early enough he ought to catch the minister before he went anywhere.

* * *

While eating breakfast, Stacey discovered her mother had several friends who attended Pastor Love's church. It took only one phone call for Stacey to learn that there was a Mrs. Love and the number of the parsonage where the Loves resided.

A breathless, sweet-sounding voice answered on the first ring, "This is Hannah."

Stacey quickly introduced herself. "I'd like to come and talk to you as soon as possible, Mrs. Love."

A startled "Oh" was followed by a long silence.

"Mrs. Love?"

"I'm wondering why you want to talk to me, Officer Wilbur."

"It's about Mallory Cookmeyer."

Again there was nothing. "Mrs. Love? Are you still there?"

"Yes, but I can't imagine why you'd want to talk to me about Mallory. I have a rather full morning."

"When is your first appointment?" Stacey asked.

The answer came reluctantly, "Nine."

"What if I come right now?"

"Well...ah...I suppose."

Stacey assured her she'd be there in fifteen minutes. Clara raised an eyebrow at her and glanced at Davey who was eating a bowl of Cheerios with banana slices.

"Mom, would you mind? This is really important?"

"Sure, I'll take Davey to school. Is it okay with you, sweetheart?"

Davey nodded. "Sure."

"It might be a good idea if you planned on picking him up too." Stacey shrugged into the jacket of her light green linen suit. She'd decided her interviewing might go better if she wasn't in uniform. "I've got a couple of places I need to go this morning, and I'm not sure how long it's going to take."

"Isn't this one of your days off, dear?" Clara asked.

"Yes, but I'll get overtime. I'm helping Doug with the Cookmeyer case."

"Good, I'm glad you're doing what you can to find out who killed Mallory," Clyde said from behind his newspaper.

"I should be able to spend most of the afternoon and evening with you, Davey, okay?"

"Sure, Mom." He still seemed preoccupied with his breakfast.

She bent down and kissed his cheek. "See you later, sweetie."

"Aren't you going to finish eating?" Clara asked.

"No, Mom. I need to get on this."

Though she'd promised Doug she would interview

Sally Jo Roberts, she felt that talking to Hannah Love might be the most urgent. She'd track Sally Jo down later.

The parsonage supplied by All Saint's Calvary Church was a far cry from the Cookmeyers' magnificent home. Located downtown, next to the parking lot behind the brick church, it was a two-story stucco and frame house built in the '30s. The front porch held wooden pots overflowing with flowering plants. Freshly painted gray with blue trim and sporting a new roof, the home contrasted sharply with its run-down neighbors.

Stacey parked her VW bug next to the curb and hurried up the steps toward the front door. Before she reached it, it flew open. She was greeted by a woman about her own size, her long nearly orange-colored hair swept back from her pale, freckled face and tied with a multi-colored scarf. She blinked pale blue eyes several times. "Are you...? I mean, I was expecting..."

Opening her shoulder bag, Stacey pulled out her wallet and displayed her ID and badge. "Hi, Mrs. Love? I'm Officer Wilbur."

Hannah took time to read the information on the ID, something few people did. "Well. I suppose you want to come in?"

Stacey smiled. "Thank you, that would be nice."

Before she allowed Stacey to enter, Hannah glanced at her watch and said, "I really do have several things I must do this morning."

"Me too. This won't take long, I promise you."

The door opened into the living room. It was crowded with comfortable looking, over-stuffed chairs and sofas filled with pillows made with of various fabrics and laces. Odd shaped tables were tucked into corners, holding ceramic lamps with fluted shades. Framed photographs of Hannah and a man Stacey guessed was Pastor Love were displayed on nearly ever surface.

One photo in particular intrigued her. It was of a young Hannah, and Joshua Love, who was thinner than he was in the other pictures, but he also wore a police uniform.

Hannah noted Stacey's interest and said, "Joshua was an L. A. police officer when we first met."

"What made him change jobs?" Stacey asked.

"He became a Christian about a year after we married and almost immediately was called into the ministry." Hannah fiddled with her fingers. "Won't you have a seat?"

Stacey settled into one of the plump chairs covered in flowered and ruffled Chintz. "How did you feel about that?"

Still standing, Hannah seemed more at ease. "Actually, I was relieved. No offense, Officer Wilbur, but I didn't much like his working hours or the dangerous nature of his job."

"What brought you to Rocky Bluff?"

"Joshua wanted to pastor a church in a small town and as soon as he finished his schooling, we started looking around. All Saints was the biggest church in Rocky Bluff back then. We visited and learned the pastor was retiring soon. Joshua offered his services as interim pastor, and one thing led to another, and we've been here ever since."

"Do you like it here?"

A shadow darkened Hannah's eyes momentarily. "It's had its ups and downs, like any job."

Stacey had the feeling pursuing that subject wouldn't lead anywhere. Instead, she asked, "Do you and Pastor Love have any children?"

Surprisingly, Hannah's bottom lip quivered. She swallowed hard several times, and a tear slid down her freckled cheek. "We had a little girl." She sniffed and fumbled in the pocket of her jumper for a tissue. Dabbing at her nose, she continued, "Kimberly Ann. Such a sweetheart." Despite the tears, Hannah smiled.

"What happened?" Stacey asked quietly.

"She had Down Syndrome and there was something wrong with her heart. The doctor recommended surgery. She died on the operating table."

She blew her nose. "Would you like to see her picture?"

"Of course."

Hannah sat on the couch and opened a large, fabric and lace covered scrapbook on the coffee table in front of her. Stacey moved next to her.

The first page held the newborn's picture taken in the hospital, along with several of Hannah and Joshua holding the infant. She looked like any other newborn, red-faced and squinty. But on the subsequent pages, Kimberly's features began to display Down Syndrome characteristics.

"This was the last picture we had taken before the surgery," Hannah said. A smiling Kimberly Ann with a mass of curly red hair, dressed in a frilly pale green dress, cuddled a teddy bear to her plump cheek.

"She was a cutie," Stacey said. "I have a little boy. He's five. I can't imagine life without him."

"It's been so hard, especially since Joshua wouldn't try again to have another child. He was afraid we'd have another child with Down Syndrome. The doctor assured him the odds were against it, but he didn't want to take the chance."

"What a shame," Stacey said, wishing she had some wiser words of comfort.

"I know you didn't come about my little girl." Hannah closed the scrapbook.

"No, I didn't. I wanted to talk to you about Mallory Cookmeyer. You did know she was dead?"

Hannah nodded. "Yes, Joshua told me yesterday. That's where he is today, planning her funeral."

"How well did you know Mallory?"

"Not well at all. She was kind of stand-offish at times, though certainly not with my husband."

Stacey stared at Hannah. "What do you mean?"

"Oh, goodness, you misunderstood. I meant that she obviously wasn't that way with Joshua because he was counseling her."

"Counseling her? Do you know why?"

She smiled sweetly. "Of course not. Their sessions

were confidential."

"Surely you had some idea what it was all about."

"Oh, I made lots of guesses. Sometimes I was even a little jealous. Though that was foolish of me. But truly, I had no way of knowing what her problem was. Joshua would never discuss private matters like that with me or anyone else." Hannah stared at her watch and sighed. "I'm so sorry, but I must be going now. I'm already late."

She stood and held her hand out to Stacey. "I'm sorry I couldn't be of any help to you. But like I said, I really didn't know Mallory or her husband very well."

Stacey squeezed Hannah's hand, thanked her and left. During the entire visit, she had the feeling that Hannah was holding back, that she was on the verge of revealing something. As much as Stacey would like to know what it was, she couldn't force Mrs. Love to tell.

Next she planned to make a surprise visit. She'd gotten Sally Jo Robert's address out of the church directory, and her father told her that the woman drove a red Toyota Camry. If it wasn't too late when she got through, maybe she'd pop into the station and give Doug a run-down on what she'd learned.

✳ ✳ ✳

Even though it wasn't yet eight by the time Doug reached the Cookmeyer residence, Reverend Cookmeyer wasn't at home. Doug found him in his office at the church. Not wasting time on pleasantries, Doug immediately sprang the coroner's findings on him.

The man leaped up from behind his desk. "Pregnant? That's impossible."

It was quite evident by his reaction that Doug's news about Mrs. Cookmeyer had come as a big shock.

"I'm afraid it's true," Doug said.

Cookmeyer ran his fingers through his thick white hair, mussing it. "But you don't understand. We couldn't have children. Goodness knows we tried. It just didn't happen."

"The truth remains, your wife was about three months pregnant at the time of her death."

He leaned across his desk, "What does this mean? Are you trying to tell me my wife was having an affair with someone? I don't believe it."

"I'm not trying to tell you anything more than the facts as I know them."

"But if she was pregnant...oh, no. Surely not. Oh, that crazy beast. He must have raped her. Why didn't she tell me? I should have reported him, even though she didn't want me to. I bet he's the one who killed her."

"Wait a minute here. Who are you talking about?"

Chapter 5

Ryan adjusted his tie, ran a hand lightly over his dark, carefully combed and sprayed hair even though he knew every strand was in place, smiled broadly and moved close to the microphone set up in the entrance to the police department. TV and newspaper reporters crowded the stairs and the sidewalk, their cameras pointed in his direction.

Though everyone else in the department hated talking to the media, Ryan was in his glory. He'd always loved the attention, and even when he was a street cop he'd managed to be interviewed by the papers and TV many times resulting in a pile of clippings for his scrapbooks. He no longer had to keep them up. Barbara had taken over that chore with great delight. He also knew she would tape this press briefing.

"Ladies and gentlemen," he began. "Though I'm sure most of you have already heard, I have the sad duty of announcing that on Saturday night, Mallory Cookmeyer, was found dead. She was the wife of Reverend Paul Cookmeyer, the minister of Rocky Bluff Community Church. Each of you will receive a handout with the facts as we know them at this time."

A written statement of information about the case had been prepared by Detectives Milligan and Marshall and approved by Chief McKenzie. One of the uniformed officers assigned to keep the gathering orderly began passing them around.

"Who did it?" one of the reporters from the Rocky Bluff Banner shouted.

"At this time we have no suspects."

Though Ryan had anticipated the first question, he didn't expect the next.

A popular and glamorous news anchor asked," Was this a crime of passion? Or perhaps a serial killer?"

"The answer to your second question is absolutely not. As to the first one, we aren't far enough along in our investigation to know." Only the information that wouldn't harm the case could be given out. "As things progress, we will keep you informed."

Ryan stepped back from the microphone.

"What about Reverend Cookmeyer?" A television reporter from a Los Angeles-based station shouted. "Where was he at the time his wife was killed? Was their marriage in trouble?" He pointed his microphone in Ryan's direction.

"At this moment, I don't have any answers. Be assured, as soon as I do, I'll pass along the information."

More questions were tossed after him, but he ignored them all, flashing one last dazzling smile in the direction of the cameras.

* * *

Before the preacher answered Doug's question,

Katherine Danfelt poked her head in the door and glowered at the detective. But when she spoke to her boss, her voice oozed sweetness. "Don't forget your appointment with Pastor Love, Reverend Cookmeyer. He'll be here soon."

"Yes, Katherine, I remember. Close the door please."

The secretary cast one last distasteful glance in Doug's direction before doing as Cookmeyer asked.

"I don't think she likes me," Doug said.

"Katherine's over-protective. She's been my secretary ever since the church could afford one. She thinks I couldn't get along without her." He chuckled. "I'm afraid that's true." He glanced at his watch. "She's also right about my appointment with Joshua. He's coming to help plan Mallory's funeral." His eyes filled with tears.

"I'm not leaving until you tell me who you were talking about."

Cookmeyer composed himself. "There was a man...came to our church for a long time...who was bothering Mallory."

"What do you mean by 'bothering'?"

"I didn't think much about it, at first. He acted like he had a crush on Mallory. That happens to me a lot with our female members. Over the years, I've learned how to discourage them. Katherine has been a great help with that. Mallory is...was a beautiful woman. I'm surprised it didn't happen to her more often."

Doug listened impatiently, wishing the minister would get to the point.

"But this fellow persisted. He started lurking around our home, and he called her on the phone. Pestered her all the time. Then he began following her."

"Did you report this?"

"Oh, I threatened to, but Mallory wouldn't let me. She felt sorry for him. Thought he had mental problems. To tell you the truth, I think she was a flattered by his interest."

"Do you know this man's name?" Doug wasn't sure whether or not to believe Cookmeyer. He could be making up the whole story to take the focus off himself. Mrs. Cookmeyer was no longer around to verify it.

"Of course I do, Detective. For goodness sake, you don't think I'm lying do you? I don't tell lies." Cookmeyer's face darkened.

Though Doug didn't consider himself a liar either, he did bend the truth when necessary—and he suspected Cookmeyer did too. This was one of those necessary times. "Of course I don't, Reverend."

"Louis Beltran, that's his name. On your way out, ask Katherine for his address and phone number."

Doug knew that was a signal for him to leave, but he wasn't quite ready. He wanted to know more about Beltran. "You're telling me that your wife put up with this guy stalking her?"

"She did for a long time, yes, far longer than I would have. Or that I wanted her to. You need to understand, Beltran is a needy sort, and my wife was a nurturing person. You'll see what I mean about Beltran when you meet him. Or maybe you won't. Whatever it is about him works mostly on women. Frankly, he seems like a bizarre-acting nerd to me. I was surprised he had the gumption to be so persistent, even after Mallory finally rebuffed him."

Doug leaned forward. "Oh? How did she do that?"

The minister shrugged. "I'm not sure exactly. She just told me that she'd taken care of the problem."

"Did she tell you how he reacted?"

"Yes, she said he got very angry, even threatened to kill her."

"Really?" Was this another attempt by Cookmeyer to throw Doug off track? "When did this happen?"

"Not too long ago, though I know Mallory didn't take the threat seriously. She thought she'd hurt him so badly that he was merely striking back verbally."

"This brings us back to the fact that you've suggested that Louis Beltran may have raped your wife.

Don't you think she'd have told you if that happened?"

"Well, yes. Except she was adamant about me not reporting this man to the police." He shook his head.

"Remember, Reverend, the coroner says Mrs. Cookmeyer was three months pregnant. She couldn't have kept this secret too much longer."

"I'm finding it difficult to believe."

"Are you positive it couldn't have been yours?"

He frowned. "To be honest, I always thought it was Mallory's fault that we never had children."

"You never had any tests done?" Doug asked.

"Well, no." Cookmeyer looked uncomfortable. "We considered it God's will that we were childless. I was positive I didn't have a problem."

"Obviously it wasn't your wife." Doug thought for a moment. "But you know it is possible it just took a long time for it to happen."

Shaking his head sadly, Cookmeyer said, "No, it wasn't my child."

A knock came at the door, and Mrs. Danfelt stepped in without waiting for an invitation. "Pastor Love is here."

Cookmeyer rose quickly and extended his hand. "If there's anything else I can help you with..."

Doug shook his hand, knowing the minister was relieved to have the interview concluded. Without a fertility test, the only way he could know positively that he wasn't the father of his wife's child was if they hadn't been having sexual relations.

* * *

Abel was dying to know what was going on with the Cookmeyer case, but he was stuck at home taking care of his little girl, Lupita. Though his mother would gladly baby-sit, it would make Maria mad. His wife and his mother didn't get along too well. His mother was extremely old-fashioned and didn't believe women should work outside of the home. It had been a constant problem while Maria was going to school and hadn't gotten any better now that she worked full-time as a nurse.

The situation was aggravated because Abel worked evenings and took care of their daughter and home during the daytime. Whenever Maria was around his family, which wasn't often, his mother made rude comments about her not fulfilling her duties as a wife and mother. She found fault with his brothers' wives too, giving Maria plenty of company.

Despite Lupita's protests, Abel switched to the mid-morning news and watched Ryan Strickland make his brief announcement.

Lupita jumped up and down. Her huge eyes were shaped like Maria's, but the color was a unique green, a mixing of her father's blue and mother's brown. Her skin wasn't as light as Abel's nor as dark as Maria's. Her long, deep brown hair was scooped up in a pony tail and fastened with her favorite Pocahontas' clip, the only hair-do Abel could manage successfully.

"I wanna see my program. Mommy always lets me watch it."

"Shhh, sweetheart, it'll only be for a minute. Daddy wants to hear his friend." He pulled the three-year-old to him, hugging her while his attention was on the screen.

Though he'd known all along he wouldn't hear anything earth shattering, Abel was disappointed that Strickland revealed less than what had been rumored around the police station yesterday evening. Abel was off tonight and tomorrow night and wouldn't dare leave Maria and Lupita.

He sighed. "Okay, sweetie, you can have your television show on now."

Somehow, he had to find out what was going on.

* * *

Sally Jo Roberts lived in a fairly new, gated-community near the beach. Stacey wondered how she could afford it. The security guard approached her car when she pulled up. "I'm here to see Sally Jo Roberts."

Before he could protest that Ms. Roberts had no visitors scheduled, Stacey opened her wallet and displayed her identification. "Official business."

Without comment, the guard stepped back inside his booth and pushed the button that opened the gate.

The choir director's home was a single story at the end of a triplex. Located near the tennis courts, it didn't have an ocean view. Stacey wondered if that meant it was cheaper.

Sally Jo opened the door as Stacey rang the bell. Dressed in a sleeveless top and short skirt, with a bag slung over her shoulder, it was obvious she was on her way out. Brushing her long, blonde hair away from her face, her eyes wide, she gasped, "Oh. I wasn't expecting anyone."

"You probably don't recognize me though I do go to the same church as you do."

Sally Jo frowned. "No, I'm afraid…"

"I don't attend all that often." Stacey opened her wallet to show her badge and identification. "Officer Wilbur, Rocky Bluff P.D. I'd like to ask you a few questions."

"Oh, well, I was on my way out. What's this about?"

"Mallory Cookmeyer's murder."

"Why would you want to ask me? For goodness, sake. Surely you don't think I had anything to do with it."

"Why don't we go inside? This won't take long."

Obviously shaken, Sally Jo stepped back so Stacey could enter the tiled foyer. Though small, the condo seemed spacious because of cathedral ceilings and the open layout. The kitchen, dining and living areas were divided only by built-in cabinets and the modern furniture. A mahogany baby grand with sheet music scattered over the lid dominated the space. A hallway opening from the side of the foyer probably led to bedrooms and bath.

Pointing toward a sitting area with a love seat and two chairs upholstered in an abstract pastel pattern, Sally Jo said, "I can't think of anything I could possibly know that could be the slightest bit helpful."

Stacey smiled at her, and sat in one of the chairs pointed out by Sally Jo. The furniture faced closed drapes with a smaller window above it that let in an abundance of light.

Noticing where Stacey was looking, Sally Jo said, "My view is across the lawn to the condos opposite mine. That's why the drapes are closed. I don't care to watch my neighbors, and I certainly don't want them watching me."

Nodding, Stacey asked, "How well did you know Mallory Cookmeyer?"

"Of course I knew her, but we weren't best friends or anything. She was a very private person. I don't think she had any close friends."

"What about her husband? What kind of relationship do you have with him?"

Sally Jo's face turned pink. "Of course I know him better. I am the choir director, after all."

"Yes, I know that." Stacey paused before springing her next question. "Do you realize that people at church are saying that you and Reverend Cookmeyer are having an affair?"

Sally Jo's face changed from pink to crimson "I...well...that isn't true."

"Why would anyone come to that conclusion?"

Dropping her gaze to her hands in her lap, Sally Jo said, "I care for Paul very deeply. He's a wonderful man. He helped me through the most difficult time in my life."

She lifted her chin and gazed directly at Stacey.

"But our relationship has not progressed beyond friendship, no matter what anyone might say."

Stacey smiled at her. "I believe you. I have the feeling that you wish it had though."

"It doesn't matter what I wish, does it?"

"Not in this situation. But the more I know, the more I can pass along to the detectives in charge of the case to convince them that what you're telling me is the truth."

Sally Jo leaned closer to Stacey. "I don't suppose it will matter if I tell you that I love Paul. At times, I think he returns my love, but he has done nothing tangible to reveal his feelings. I catch a glimpse in his eyes or his expression when we're together, but that's all, I swear. Maybe I'm reading more into that than is really there. You see, he saved my life."

Chapter 6

Louis Beltran's owlish eyes grew even rounder behind his plastic-framed glasses when Doug explained why he was there. Doug located him easily. He worked for a local Internet server in a former dress shop in the old downtown district. Surrounded by computers and printers, Beltran awkwardly unfolded his lanky frame to greet Doug at a makeshift counter littered with books, folders stuffed with papers, and computer disks and CDs.

Long, pale arms extended from his short-sleeved plaid shirt, and he swiped nervously at the dark hair stringing down over his narrow forehead. "Why do you want to know what I was doing Saturday night?"

"Is it so difficult to tell me where you were and what you were up to?"

He chewed at a fingernail. "No, of course not, but I can't help but wonder, is all."

"Why don't you tell me, and then we'll go from there."

Somewhere in his late twenties, Beltran was neither homely nor handsome. Perhaps if he got a decent haircut and more modern glasses, shaved a little closer and wore something besides his nondescript shirt and baggy pants he might even be good-looking. "I was here answering phones. Helping people with their computer problems, like I do most evenings."

"Anybody here with you?"

"Uh-uh."

"Have you any way to prove that you were here?"

Beltran blinked several times. "Actually, I do." He stepped over to one of the computers, picked up a loose-leaf binder and plopped it down on the counter. After flipping through a couple of pages, he turned the binder around and pointed out the date with a long, knobby finger. "See, this is Saturday. I log in every call I get, the time, who it's from, the nature of the problem, and how it was resolved."

Doug scanned the log. If accurate, Beltran was busy during the time of Mallory Cookmeyer's murder. Phone numbers were listed alongside each name. "Can I have a copy of this?"

"Sure." Using a copier near the back of the room, Beltran did as he was asked.

When he handed the sheet of paper over to Doug, he asked, "Now are you going to tell me what this is about?"

"I'm investigating the murder of Mrs. Mallory Cookmeyer. I understand that you..."

Before Doug could finish, Beltran staggered backwards, and gasped, "What? Mallory is dead? Are you sure? What happened?"

Frowning, Doug asked, "You didn't know? It's been in the papers and on TV."

"Oh, my God. I can't believe it." Tears poured from his eyes, and he collapsed in the chair beside the computer. "It can't be true."

"I'm sorry, but it is," Doug said kindly.

Beltran wiped his face and blew his nose with a handkerchief he fished from the pocket of his trousers. He peered myopically at Doug. "You came here because you thought...oh, oh, oh...I'd never do anything to harm her." He shook his head slowly. "I loved her."

"The Reverend Cookmeyer told me that you stalked her, and when she rebuffed you, you threatened her life."

Leaping back to his feet, Beltran exclaimed, "But I didn't mean it. I was so hurt that I didn't know what I was saying."

"Then it's true? You did stalk her?"

"No, no, I wasn't stalking. I only wanted to be near her."

"But you did know she was married."

"Yes, of course, but Reverend Cookmeyer didn't give her the attention she deserved. He spent all his time with other women."

"Are you saying that her husband was unfaithful to her?"

"Not in the way you mean, but she was left alone so much. When she had a problem, she went to another minister for help."

"How do you know?"

Beltran took a long time answering. "Because I followed her."

"What minister did she see?"

"Pastor Love. You've got to understand, she was a wonderful woman. She'd never have gone to him for help if her husband had paid any attention to her."

The phone rang. Beltran glanced toward it.

"Go ahead and answer. I think I've got everything I need for now."

* * *

"Chief McKenzie wants to see you as soon as possible," were the first words out of Clara's mouth when Stacey returned home.

"Did he say what he wanted?" Stacey asked.

"No, just that he'd like you to come in for a chat."

"A chat? That was the word he used?"

Clara nodded. "Yes, I thought that rather strange too."

"I planned to go to the station anyway to tell Doug what I found out."

"I hope nothing is wrong," Clara said.

"It's probably something about this murder case." Maybe the Chief found out Stacey was helping Doug with the murder investigation on her own time and wanted her to stop. "I better go."

"Don't worry, dear, we'll look after Davey."

Thank God for her parents. At least Davey could count on them.

* * *

With Lupita's dimpled hand firmly in his, Abel walked through the front entrance of the department. Pointing at the several chairs, he said, "This is where people wait."

He lifted Lupita and sat her down on the front counter. "These are the ladies who help everyone." On the other side of the glass separating the lobby from the reception desks, sat two female public safety officers, with the dispatchers' modules beyond.

Trained volunteers, the public safety officers wore black and white uniforms and worked in the field answering non-threatening calls as well as manning the reception area. Lydia Morales, one of the women on duty, came to the glass and slid open the window. "Hi, Sergeant. This must be your little girl."

"Sure is, this is Lupita. We're on a field trip to see

where Daddy works."

Lupita grinned at Lydia.

Lydia said, "Hi, sweetie. I'll buzz you in."

The door to the inside unlocked. Abel swung Lupita into his arms, and entered. Keeping up his pretense, he introduced his daughter to the dispatchers and explained what they did. He pointed out his desk in the office that he shared with several others, the squad room with its posters, maps, rows of chairs, and the door to the Chief's office. He was surprised to see Stacey Wilbur, dressed in civilian clothes, disappear inside.

He cheerily greeted the uniformed officer he encountered, each one taking the time to speak to Lupita. When he reached the homicide detectives' office, he knocked on the door, hoping to find either Doug or Frank inside.

"Come in," Doug's voice rang out.

Abel poked his head in. "Busy? I'm showing my little girl around the station."

"Working on the Cookmeyer murder."

"How's it going?" Abel stepped inside the small room, and pulled up a chair. Doug had an open folder filled with papers in front of him.

"Don't know a whole lot yet. Hi, Lupita. How are you, sweetie?" He raised an eyebrow. "You might not want your little girl to hear what I do know."

"Oh, yeah, right." Abel swung Lupita into his arms. "Let's see if we can find one of the nice ladies to give you a doughnut and maybe a soda. What do you say?"

When he returned alone, Doug said, "The most interesting things so far is probably the fact that the victim was pregnant and her husband didn't know it."

"Wow, that is something. You think maybe she was having an affair with someone?"

"It's a possibility. The husband thought she might have been raped by this computer nerd who'd been stalking her."

"Do you think he did it?"

"He has an alibi, and it seems to be checking out."

"If not him, then who is your favorite suspect? The husband?"

"So far, he's all I've got. But I sent Stacey out to interview someone, I'm anxious to hear what she found out."

"I saw her going into the Chief's office a minute ago."

Doug seemed startled by the news. "Really?"

"Yeah."

"Wonder what that's about?"

* * *

Chief McKenzie looked more like a bank president than the head of a police department. From behind his desk, he peered at Stacey over his wire-rimmed glasses perched mid-way down his nose. As always, he wore a suit, dress shirt and tie, his graying hair cut short. He seemed to be studying Stacey as she sat on the opposite side of his large, mahogany desk.

Finally, he spoke. "This morning a woman came in and wouldn't talk to anyone but me. Turns out, she's a prostitute. We've arrested her several times. She had quite a story and wants our help."

Stacey couldn't imagine what this had to do with her.

McKenzie's folded his hands in front of him on the shiny surface of his desk. "It seems. she was approached by a man who was looking for a young girl for sexual purposes. He was specific, the child had to be under ten. He offered the woman quite a sum to set it up for him. Told her he's done it before, and then took her to his car and showed her a book of pictures of him having sex with a young girl."

"How awful," Stacey said, unable to prevent a shudder.

"Yes, it is. The reason this prostitute came to us with this is because she wants to keep it from happening, and she'd like the perpetrator put away."

"Yes, sir." Stacey still wondered what it had to do with her.

"Since you are the only female officer on the department at this time, I'd like to enlist your assistance. You are not obligated to say yes. We'd like to keep from turning the investigation over to an outside agency, and the only way we can do a successful operation is to have a female officer pose as a prostitute willing to sell her daughter for sex."

Stacey's heart took a tumble. She felt torn. Of course, she wanted to get this man off the streets, but could she play the part of someone capable of doing such a vile thing to her own child?

"Think about it. I know it's a difficult decision. We'll set it up carefully, you'll have a wire and be under surveillance the whole time."

"I don't know, sir." Could she even pull it off? "I suppose I could make myself up to look like a prostitute, but I don't know if I could act like a mother who would do such a thing. It's so sick."

"Don't worry, we'll write a script. Tell you exactly what you have to say to this guy. You have to be careful so he can't plead entrapment. He's got to ask for what he wants, you can't offer it."

"Yes, sir, I know."

"We'd like to keep the investigation in our department."

"I understand." She really did. If she turned down the job, they'd have to ask the county sheriff to take over and since this man was operating in Rocky Bluff, it would be a blow to their department. If she agreed, she wouldn't be able to help Doug with the Cookmeyer case until this new case was resolved.

"I really would like to help catch this monster..." Stacey began.

"Terrific."

"But, I've interviewed a couple of people about the Cookmeyer murder for Detective Milligan and I haven't had a chance to fill him in as yet."

McKenzie smiled. "No problem. You bring Milligan up to speed, and I'll organize a group of officers for this operation. I'll contact our informant so she can set up a meet between you and our suspect."

He sounded like it was all settled though Stacey didn't feel like she'd given him an affirmative answer. She knew deep in her heart, that no matter how abhorrent it might be to come in contact with this pervert, or how scary it might be to act like someone she wasn't, she would do anything possible to keep this man from hurting another little girl.

* * *

After greeting Stacey with a kiss, Doug asked, "Abel told me he saw you going into the Chief's office. What was that all about?"

"I'll tell you later. Right now, I have a lot of information for you about Sally Jo Roberts. I also talked to Hannah Love, the pastor's wife."

"Did this Roberts woman admit to having an affair with Cookmeyer?"

Stacey shook her head. "No, she said they aren't romantically involved, but she did admit to being in love with him."

"Which means she could have wanted Mrs. Cookmeyer dead."

"She told me that Reverend Cookmeyer saved her life."

"How'd he do that?"

"She was in an extremely abusive marriage. She went to Cookmeyer for help. He encouraged her to leave her husband. He took her to a shelter, dealt with the husband, and guided her through the divorce. She's convinced if he hadn't intervened, her husband would have eventually killed her."

"H'mm, that's interesting," Doug said.

After Stacey filled him in on all she'd learned from the choir director, she moved on to her visit with Hannah Love. "Did you know that Pastor Love was once an L.A.P.D. officer?"

"News to me."

"Something else I learned was that he was counseling Mallory Cookmeyer and his wife wasn't too happy about it." She filled him in on the meeting, about Mrs. Love's dead child, and her husband's unwillingness to have another, and her jealousy toward Mallory.

Doug took notes as Stacey spoke. When she'd finished, he asked, "What were your general feelings about Hannah Love?"

"Though she was quite candid about some areas of her life, I felt that she was holding back. You probably ought to talk to her."

Doug glanced at his watch. "Have you had lunch yet?"

"No, but I really should be getting home. I'd like to spend some time with Davey this evening, and I have some shopping to do."

"You aren't leaving without telling me what Chief McKenzie wanted."

"He wants me to dress up like a prostitute to trap a pedophile."

"A ridiculous idea. There is no way you could be mistaken for a prostitute. What could the Chief be thinking? You aren't going to do it, are you?"

She nodded. "Yes, I guess I am."

Chapter 7

"Me and daddy went to the police station," Lupita told her mother at the exact moment Maria entered the house.

"What? Abel, is that true?" Maria's dark eyes blazed.

"We went on a field trip. Lupita wanted to see where I worked. It was fun." Abel moved close to Maria to kiss her mouth, but she quickly turned her head so his lips landed on her cheek.

"Oh, Abel, I know you too well. You went to the station to find out what was going on with that murder case. Admit it. But to take our innocent little girl around all those horrible criminals..."

"It wasn't like that at all, honey. We didn't see a single bad guy. It was quiet today. We weren't there for more than thirty minutes."

"Honestly." She shook her head and frowned.

"Why aren't you in uniform? Aren't you working tonight?"

Usually Maria arrived home from her job only a few minutes before Abel left to go to his.

"Got the night off. I'm going to be on special assignment tomorrow."

"What's that all about?"

"Can't tell you until it's over." He leaned near her again, and this time she pressed her lips against his, but quickly pulled away.

Pouting, she said, "Darn, that means your mother will be babysitting Lupita."

"Yes, but it's okay, I don't have to go in until eight, I can drop Lupita off."

Maria's face softened. "Did you make anything for supper?"

* * *

After a long day of interviewing people and making phone calls, Doug and Frank met in their office to compare notes.

"What about this stalker, Louis Beltran," Frank asked, tipping back in his chair. "He certainly fits the profile for a murder like this."

"Yeah, and to tell you the truth, I was hoping he'd be the one. But I checked his alibi." He tossed the sheet of paper with the list of phone calls, times, and numbers across the desk in Frank's direction. "Like he said, he was talking on the phone to these people during the time of the murder."

"Maybe he used a cell phone," Frank suggested. "Then he could have taken care of business while he went anywhere he wanted."

"I thought of that...suggested it to a couple of these people when I talked to them, but each one said it wasn't possible. The help he was giving them was tied into what he was doing at the computer. Seems Louis Beltran's only crime was making a pest out of himself with Mallory Cookmeyer. He admitted threatening her but said he didn't mean it, and I'm inclined to believe him. He got his job with an Internet provider about the same time Reverend Cookmeyer threatened to turn him in. His love of computers seems to be more powerful than the crush he had on Mrs. Cookmeyer."

"Okay, so that brings us back to the husband who doesn't have an alibi at all. Do we have a motive?" Frank asked.

"Maybe. The fact that Mallory was pregnant and Cookmeyer seemed genuinely shocked by the news suggests that there may have been another man in her life."

Frank sat up straight. "Any idea who?"

"From the information Stacey brought me, it might be Pastor Love."

Frank grinned. "Oh, yeah?"

"We haven't got anything concrete. Love was counseling Mallory, and his wife was jealous of her. Stacey felt Mrs. Love was keeping something back so I suppose we'll have to lean on her a bit."

"Funeral is tomorrow morning," Frank said. "We should go and pay our respects. Funerals always seem to provide lots of useful information."

"I'm curious about this Pastor Love too. Stacey found out he used to be on the L.A. Police Department."

"Quite a switch, to go from cop to preacher."

"I think we ought to check him out. Find out something about his record when he was on the job."

"I'll do that in the morning. I've got some pals down there that owe me."

Doug got up and stretched. "And there's the choir director. Pretty little Sally Jo."

"You think she's a suspect?"

"Could be. She's in love with Rev. Cookmeyer. Denies that they're having an affair even though the church gossips think there's one going on."

"If the Reverend returned the feelings, it makes his motive stronger. I have some information about the fingerprints we got out of the car."

"Anything interesting?"

"Maybe. Of course we identified Mrs. Cookmeyer's and the Reverend's, but there were three distinct prints that we don't have any matches for. We need to run them through a bigger data base. I'll get that going before I leave."

"We need to get a set of Sally Jo's and Hannah Love's prints too."

"My thoughts exactly." Frank scribbled in a notebook and stood. "And there's someone else we ought to print."

"Who's that?"

"With Reverend Cookmeyer's permission, I spent some time in his office today, looking through his appointment book and his desk. Didn't find anything interesting, by the way, but that secretary of his is a nasty old broad. She would hardly give me the time-of-day. I think she needs to be printed too."

"Why?"

"If for no other reason than to shake her up a bit."

Doug laughed.

* * *

Stacey spent the evening with Davey and her folks. They played three games of Sorry—Davey won every time—and watched one of his favorite videos. After his bath, she read him a story, heard his prayers and tucked him into bed. Before joining her folks in the living room, she once again examined the purchases she'd made that afternoon.

Shaking her head, she knew that she would have to explain to her parents what was going on before she dressed for her assignment tomorrow.

They were settled into their matching recliners in front of the television; Stacey stepped in front of the screen. "Would you mind turning that off for a few minutes. I have something important to tell you."

Clyde picked up the remote and turned off the set. He moved his chair to a sitting position. "What is it? You sound serious."

Clara's eyes opened wide. "Oh, goodness. Has something happened?"

"It's about my job," Stacey began.

"Dear me, is this about that meeting with Chief McKenzie?" Clara's face expressed worry.

"Yes, it is. He asked me to be a part of an undercover operation."

Clara gasped." Good heavens."

"That sounds dangerous," Clyde said.

"It really isn't dangerous though it is rather distasteful," Stacey explained. "I can't tell you what it's all about until it's over, but I did want to warn you." She paused trying to think what she wanted to say and how to say it.

"Warn us? Oh, my." Clara's hand flew to her bosom.

"What I mean, Mom, is I have to dress up in a bizarre outfit tomorrow and I didn't want to shock you."

"What do you mean by 'bizarre'?" her father asked.

"I'm going to be posing as a prostitute."

Clara's hand flew to her mouth and Clyde's white eyebrows shot upward.

"You aren't going to have to do anything..." Clara began.

"No, no, don't worry, I don't have to be a hooker, but I do have to look and act like one. I wanted to prepare you."

"I don't understand why do you have to do this." Clara said.

"I'm sorry, Mom, I really can't explain. I'll tell you more when it's over. What I can say, is that it's really important."

"Of course, honey," Clyde said. "You have to do your job."

"Will you want us to take care of Davey?" Clara asked.

"That was the next thing I had to discuss. I need to go in early, and I have no idea when I'll be back. So if I can count on you to tend to Davey that will really help."

"Of course," Clara said, "you know we will. But I can't help but worry."

"Now, Clara, the girl has to do her job."

"You will be careful, won't you?"

* * *

Called to investigate a possible prowler, Gordon Butler rolled his unit with the lights off, toward the address given to him by the dispatcher. It was near the end of Tulip Drive, one of many streets that wound their way toward the foothills. An old neighborhood, before the homes were built on the bluffs, this had been the favored place to live.

Feeling his adrenalin level rising, Gordon peered through his windshield and the side window, searching for a sign of overt activity. Each house had a different architectural style, built in the twenties or earlier. Most were owned by retired people with comfortable incomes, not many children in the neighborhood, though a young family lived here and there, as evidenced by skateboards and bikes left on the front lawns.

Unfortunately, for reasons of security, yards were landscaped with trees full of foliage and plump bushes that created deep shadows. Tall plants hugged the outside walls.

At the last house from the corner, one of the shadows separated itself from the others. "Bingo."

There wasn't time to report to the dispatcher. He

couldn't let this bozo get away. Slamming on the brakes, Gordon snatched his keys from the ignition, grabbed his baton, leaped from the car leaving the door open, and ran toward the shadow that had sprouted two legs and arms and was moving quickly away from him.

"Halt." he shouted. "Police."

The suspect disappeared around the side of the house. Gordon quickened his stride, and moved around the structure in time to see the figure push through a gate in a wooden fence. Only a few yards behind, Gordon pursued him into a large backyard with a flagstone patio, several pieces of outdoor furniture, and a large fish pond.

Again, Gordon hollered, "Stop," but the suspect kept right on going. The property was bordered by a five-foot hedge and the running figure leaped over it like a track star.

"Oh boy," Gordon muttered. Pushing himself even harder, he pumped his legs, and barely sailed over the hedge.

As he cleared the neatly trimmed barrier, his stomach lurched and his heart beat quickened as he realized the ground dropped away at least six feet. He landed hard, but didn't remain upright. He tumbled forward, hitting his head on a hard surface. For a moment all he saw was a kaleidoscope of shimmering bright colors.

Chapter 8

It was nearly ten o'clock when Doug called. "I wanted to see you this evening, but I had to go to the hospital."

Stacey's heart leaped. "What's wrong? Did you get hurt? Are you sick?"

"No, no, it wasn't about me. Gordon got himself into another situation. I had to check on him in the emergency room."

Doug didn't sound upset, so she guessed it wasn't too serious. "What happened this time?"

"He was chasing a prowler and went over a hedge with a six-foot drop on the other side. He landed on his feet but lost his balance and struck his head on the sidewalk. Got a concussion for his trouble."

"Poor Gordon."

"He's more perturbed about the suspect getting away than having to spend the night in the hospital.

That brings me to my next point. I'm going to have the house to myself for a change, maybe we could get together? I know it's awfully late but…"

Stacey broke in, "Too late I'm afraid. I never got around to telling you what the Chief wanted with me. I'm going to be on special assignment tomorrow."

"Special assignment? What's that all about?"

She described it quickly.

"I'm not sure you ought to be doing this. You've never been undercover before. Sounds dangerous to me. It doesn't sound like we know enough about this guy. He could be armed."

"Don't worry, Doug, I'll have plenty of back-up."

"Yeah, I know, but I'd sure feel better if I was in on this operation."

"This guy is such a pervert. I want to do whatever I can to keep him from hurting another little girl."

Doug sighed loudly. "Obviously I can't talk you out of this."

"No, it's something I have to do. I wish I could see you."

"Me too. Be careful tomorrow."

* * *

Doug and Frank stood behind the last row of pews in the large sanctuary of Rocky Bluff Community Church. There wasn't an empty seat left and several mourners lined the polished cedar walls. Bouquets and wreaths surrounded the closed casket in front of the pulpit. Reverend Cookmeyer, easily recognizable by his white hair, sat on the end of the front pew. Next to him was a woman with red hair, perhaps Hannah Love, and down the row was the unmistakably dyed black, short coiffure of Katherine Danfelt. Doug noticed Stacey's parents seated about midway on the right-hand side. He hoped he'd have a chance to greet them.

Stained glass in an abstract design backed the choir loft. The choir, led by a petite, long-haired blonde, wore dark blue robes and were already singing a subdued "Abide in Me."

"That's Sally Jo Roberts, the choir director that's in love with Cookmeyer," Doug murmured behind his hand to Frank.

"Cute little thing."

When the choir sat down, the balding Joshua Love rose from behind the altar. Raising his arms, he spoke in sonorous tones, "Friends and loved ones, we are gathered together to celebrate the life of our sister in Christ, Mallory Christine Cookmeyer."

He went on to describe the deceased's childhood, but Doug barely listened as his eyes scanned the crowd. Handkerchiefs dabbed at eyes, noses were blown, and once in a while a stifled sob could be heard. From what he'd learned from Stacey about Mallory's stand-offishness, he imagined some of the grief was more because of her life being taken in such a violent and unexpected manner than for the actual loss.

Doug's thoughts were interrupted by Pastor Love's voice, "Mallory's life was touched by pain as a young woman when her parents were taken from her in a plane crash."

Doug and Frank exchanged glances. Interesting. Doug wondered if that had any bearing on the case.

"What a joyous reunion they must be having in heaven." Pastor Love beamed over the gathering. He appeared to be thoroughly enjoying his performance, despite the reason for it.

After the obligatory scripture readings, several more renditions by the choir and a final prayer, most of the mourners filed past Reverend Cookmeyer. He stood regal and handsome, though his expression was sad, in front of his wife's casket. Most of his congregation hugged him, openly weeping. In most cases, it looked like he was doing the consoling.

Doug and Frank moved closer to the aisle. When

Katherine Danfelt neared, Frank touched her arm. "Mrs. Danfelt, could you step outside for a moment? We'd like to talk to you."

Mrs. Danfelt scowled. "Whatever for? I'm supposed to ride in the limousine with Reverend Cookmeyer."

"This won't take long. From the look of things, your boss is going to be occupied for a while," Doug said.

"I can't believe this. You two have no sense of propriety whatsoever. But I suppose if you insist..."

"We do," Frank said. He grasped her elbow and guided her outside.

Though some people had left to get back to jobs, Doug supposed, the majority stood talking in small groups on the vast lawn and near vehicles in the parking lot. Fog had replaced the Santa Ana winds, swirling around eerily, cutting visibility to a minimum.

Frank led Mrs. Danfelt away from everyone and began immediately with the reason they wanted to talk to her. "We compared your fingerprints with those we found in Mrs. Cookmeyer's car and we discovered that some of them are yours. Do you have an explanation for that?"

"For goodness sake. Surely you don't think? Why I never... Of course, I have an explanation. I am Reverend Cookmeyer's secretary, after all. I couldn't even count the number of times I've ridden along with Mrs. Cookmeyer to some function or other. It would be more odd if my fingerprints weren't in her car." She stared from one to the other, her dark, neatly plucked eyebrows raised.

Frank said, "Reverend Cookmeyer will corroborate that?"

"Of course." Mrs. Danfelt pulled the black jacket of her pant suit around her tighter. "Can I go now? I think Reverend Cookmeyer is coming out." She started to brush past Frank but stopped abruptly. "Will you look at that? Doesn't he have any sense at all?"

Pallbearers escorted the coffin toward the hearse

parked in front of the church. With Pastor Love and his wife leading the way, Reverend Cookmeyer, with his hand on the small of her back, escorted Sally Jo Roberts toward the long, gray limousine parked behind the black hearse.

"That's who you ought to be investigating. She's always fawning over the Reverend. Despite what he told you, Sally Jo knew he was at the church on Saturday night. There was choir practice in the afternoon, and she always hangs around afterwards to see him. He didn't mention her to you in order to protect her. I've got to go now."

"Wait a minute," Frank said. "What makes you..."

Mrs. Danfelt ignored him and rushed away toward the group disappearing inside the limousine.

"That was enlightening. We'll have to talk to her some more. What she said might be a smoke screen to cover up her own actions, but it does seem rather odd that the Reverend would be so obvious about flaunting a lover so soon after his wife's death."

Doug was about to make his own observation when he spotted a tall skinny man, wearing an ill-fitting, rumpled dark suit standing near the hearse. It was Louis Beltran. Tears flowed openly down his long, narrow face.

* * *

The meet with the alleged pedophile had been arranged by the prostitute for eleven a.m. Stacey waited on the corner of Mulberry and Valley Drive in an older, run-down section of Rocky Bluff favored by prostitutes and their tricks. She was thankful for the thick fog, though it made it hard to see who was coming, it also made her less noticeable as she paced back-and-forth in her tight black mini-skirt and high-heeled sandals.

When she'd arrived at the station, she'd worn a long coat to conceal her outfit, but she'd still been greeted by startled glances and a few wolf calls. She'd lightened her hair with a blonde rinse, back-combed and teased it to give it a spiky fullness. Her make-up mimicked the prostitutes she'd arrested in the past, with lots of mascara and eye-liner and blush, outlining her lips with a brown pencil and filling them in with a dark shade of red.

As an artistic touch, she'd purchased stick-on tattoos from a local parlor and now sported a rose on her shoulder and a small heart on her ankle. Because of a push-up bra, her scooped neck, turquoise body shirt displayed more cleavage than she was comfortable with.

At their meeting, Chief McKenzie had taken one look at her and asked, "Where are we supposed to put the wire?"

Sergeant Stafford came up with the solution. Stafford, a spit-and-polish, by-the-book officer, had been recruited along with several others for this special detail. "Hook one of those wires that looks like a pager to the strap on her purse."

The pager was affixed on the shoulder strap close enough to her shoulder, so anything that was said to her would be easily transmitted to the van where the men would listen, record the conversation, and wait for her signal. Everything else was in readiness. The Chief had obtained a search warrant for the man's home and his vehicle in order to locate the album of pictures he'd shown the prostitute.

Clicking back and forth on her unaccustomed high-heels, Stacey glanced at her watch. It was ten minutes past the arranged hour. The van was around the corner and she knew the sergeant, Abel Navarro, Felix Zachary and Ryan Strickland were as anxious as she was. Stacey shivered both from the cold and nervousness. The temperature was about twenty degrees cooler than it had been the day before at the same time.

A large figure emerged out of the fog, moving quickly toward her. Stacey's heart quickened. "Someone's coming," she breathed, scarcely moving her lips.

There was something familiar about the bulky form and the loping stride. It was Gordon Butler. "Damn."

In civilian clothes, Gordon stared at her, frowning. "Hey, Stacey, is that you? Why are you dressed like that?"

Stacey quickly glanced around, hoping the suspect she waited for wasn't nearby. "I'm on special assignment. You ought to be able to figure that out by how I look.

He grinned. "Oh, yeah? What's going down?"

"I haven't got time to talk, Gordon. For crying out loud, get away from me." She turned her back on him.

He stared after her, his mouth gaping. "Oh, yeah. Hey. See you."

When she had decided her quarry had either been scared off by her encounter with Gordon or was going to be a "no-show", a silver Mercedes convertible with its top up pulled longside her.

"Hello, there." A pleasant faced man in his early forties leaned toward her. "Are you waiting for me?"

He wasn't at all what she'd expected. Even white teeth were exposed by a friendly grin. His brown hair was lightly touched with gray at the temples. He wore a tweed sport jacket, open-necked pale yellow dress shirt, and crisply creased tan slacks. He had a lodge ring on his right hand and gold wedding band on his left.

"I believe I am," she said.

He swung open the passenger door and she slid into the front seat next to him.

"We have some business to discuss," he said, staring at her carefully.

She nodded.

He dropped his hand to her bare thigh.

It was all she could do to keep herself from knocking his hand away.

He stared pointedly at the pager. "Turn that thing off."

Even though it would drive the team in the van crazy, she knew she had to do as he asked or nothing would come of the meeting. "Sure." Somehow she would have to find a reason to turn it back on without making him suspicious.

"I understand you have an eight-year-old daughter," he said. Something evil glimmered in his blue-gray eyes. Stacey knew despite the hand resting above her knee, he had no interest in her. It was all she could do not to display her disgust.

"Would you like to see a picture of her?" Stacey opened her purse. She pulled out a group of photographs generously donated by one of the dispatchers of her daughter. They depicted a blonde eight-year-old in various poses: wearing red-white-and-blue satin shorts and blouse and tasseled boots and twirling a baton, in a green-and-gray soccer uniform, blowing out eight candles on a birthday cake, and in a bikini at the beach.

He studied each picture carefully. "Delightful. Exactly what I'm looking for. What's her name?"

"Jennifer."

He went through the pictures again. "She'll do nicely. Are we agreeable on the price?"

Stacey mentioned the extremely large amount the prostitute had quoted, adding, "And exactly what do you expect for that amount?"

"Didn't the other girl tell you?"

"Of course, but I want everything up front. No surprises."

"This will be her first time, I presume," the man said.

Stacey nodded. Her mind raced. She had to turn the wire back on or this whole meeting would be wasted.

"I can assure you that it will be a good experience for her. I've done this before, you know. I'll be extremely gentle." A film of sweat appeared on his upper lip; he was already anticipating his disgusting acts.

His perversion had to be on tape before they

arrested him. An idea came to her. "Jennifer is probably trying to get in touch with me, so I'll have to turn this on now so we can go pick her up."

"Oh, sure, of course," he said eagerly, his tongue darting out to moisten his lips.

She pressed the switch on the phony pager. "Now before we do this, I have to be positive that Jennifer will be okay."

"Hey. Don't worry. I've already got a nice room at the motel. You can be there the whole time. In fact, I'd like you to take pictures." He went on to describe exactly what he planned to do to the little girl. "I assure you, I know how. I won't hurt her, I've had lots of practice."

It took all Stacey's inner strength not to show her revulsion. "What about the money?"

He reached in his pocket and pulled out a folded stack of bills. "Here's half now, and you can have the rest when I'm through."

That should do it. Using the pre-arranged signal, Stacey coughed.

The doors of a local locksmith's van burst open. The officers in riot gear exploded out of it. In seconds, Abel Navarro yanked open the passenger door and helped her out of the Mercedes while Sergeant Stafford hauled the suspect out of the other side. The Sergeant was already reading the man his rights.

Abel whisked Stacey away from the scene and to the van. "Good work, Stacey. We've got enough to make the case."

"I hoped he'd show me that book of his," Stacey said, climbing into the van. "We've got to put this slime ball away. He makes me want to vomit."

"Don't worry, we've got him."

Abel called for a waiting police unit, while Stafford and Zachary patted down the suspect and read him his rights. Strickland pocketed the keys to the Mercedes and trotted back to the van.

He grinned widely. "You did a terrific job, Wilbur. Had him fooled but good. At first he wouldn't admit to having his dirty picture book, but when we told him we had a search warrant he said it was in his house. I thought he'd lawyer up right away, but he wants to go with us. We're going over there as soon as the unit arrives. How about calling for a tow truck, Navarro? We'll have the Mercedes taken to his home. We don't dare leave a car like that in this neighborhood or it'll get stolen for sure."

While Abel arranged for the tow, Stacey asked, "Did you find out who he is?"

"Name's Evan Truesdale. He's an architect. Has his own firm here in town. Must do okay judging by his clothes and car."

"Wonder if he has a family?" Stacey asked.

A blue-and-white unit rolled to a squeaky stop. Strickland said, "We'll find out soon enough."

Chapter 9

Doug and Frank tagged along behind the long procession of vehicles following the hearse and limousine heading toward the cemetery.

"Let's go over what we know so far." Frank tapped his fingers on the steering wheel as he drove, no doubt agitated by how slow they were moving.

"Cookmeyer still looks like the prime suspect to me," Doug said. "He certainly has plenty of motive. Perhaps he was afraid everyone was going to find out about his affair with the choir director. Only way he could marry her was get rid of his wife."

"Thought Wilbur told you Miss Roberts said they weren't having an affair."

Doug snorted. "That's what she told Stacey, but she's probably lying to protect her boyfriend. Remember how upset our dear friend Katherine Danfelt was when she spotted her boss helping Sally Jo into the limo?"

"Uh huh, and our buddy also thinks we ought to be investigating the choir director, but I have some other thoughts about that."

"Go ahead."

"I can't help thinking our cranky secretary may have done away with her boss's wife. After all she is overprotective of him. She seems to know all his business, personal and private. I bet she was well aware of Mallory's affair and her pregnancy. She could have seen Mallory's death as the only way to protect Reverend Cookmeyer's reputation." Frank reached into his pocket and pulled out a stick of gum, unwrapping it while keeping one hand on the steering wheel.

"It's possible I suppose, but I still put my money on Cookmeyer."

Frank chewed his gum thoughtfully. "What about that computer fellow? Maybe we're dismissing him too soon."

"He's worth keeping an eye on, but I think his alibi will stand up. The people I called wouldn't have any reason to lie to me."

Frank chewed and steered, his eyes on the car ahead of him while Doug continued to mull over what they knew so far.

"The choir director might have done it. She could be telling the truth if she felt she had to get Mallory out of the way for Cookmeyer to pay any attention to her."

"Could be, I suppose, but do we have any evidence to support that theory?"

"No...but we haven't explored the possibility either."

Because of the long line of vehicles, there was no room to park inside Rocky Bluff's cemetery when Frank and Doug arrived. After finding a spot, they had to walk nearly a quarter mile before arriving at the grassy area where the casket reposed beside a blanket of artificial turf hiding the grave site. Many of the flowers had been transported from the church and provided a backdrop for the final gathering.

The mourners heads were bowed. Pastor Love was in the middle of a prayer. It was impossible to get close enough to hear. Frank and Doug observed the proceedings from a group of tall granite and marble monuments.

Through a break in the crowd, Doug had a perfect view of a slim woman with a black straw hat topping a cascade of bright red hair. Pastor Love's wife, Hannah. What was it Stacey had said about her?

He nudged Frank. "There's one more suspect."

Frank frowned. "Yeah, who's that?"

Doug pointed. "Hannah Love. She told Stacey that she was jealous of Mallory."

"Why?"

"Because her husband was counseling Mallory. He was spending too much time with her, I suppose."

"Doesn't sound like much to me."

"Maybe not, but the least we can do is pursue it a bit further. I'd like Stacey to do it. I think the woman might clam up if we questioned her."

"Sure, why not?"

"Might not be possible, she's on special assignment."

"I don't like it when it takes so long to nab the murderer. If we don't get some kind of break soon, this may be one of those unsolved murder cases. Chief McKenzie won't be happy about that."

✻ ✻ ✻

The unit carrying the suspect, Sergeant Stafford, and Officer Zachary, parked directly in front of Evan Truesdale's house. Officer Zachary opened the back door of the unit, grabbed the suspect by the elbow and helped him out.

Abel braked the van to a stop. Stacey and Ryan Strickland piled out immediately.

Truesdale's house was on the bluff, one of the more expensive ones perched on the cliff overlooking the ocean. It was a massive salmon-colored edifice surrounded by matching adobe walls and wrought iron gates guarding the front entrance to the house and the driveway to the garage. Warning signs were posted on both gates: BEWARE OF DOG.

Ferocious barking and growling attracted everyone's attention. A muscular Rottweiler strained against the bars of the nearest gate, his sharp teeth bared, saliva foaming.

"No one's home," Truesdale said. "You'll have to take off the cuffs so I can chain my dog."

It was obvious they'd never be able to get inside the yard unless the dog was out of the way. Zachary, the only black officer on the department, raised a questioning eyebrow in Abel's direction. Abel turned to Stafford, the senior man of the group.

"Handcuff him in front. He can tend to the dog like that." Stafford directed.

As soon as he spotted his master, the dog calmed. "It's okay, Terminator," Truesdale said in a soothing tone, as Zachary walked with him to the gate.

"Terminator, what kind of a name is that?" Zachary asked. He was known for his lack of fondness towards canines of any sort.

"I didn't have any part in it. My boys named him."

Stacey felt nauseous. The suspect had kids. Thank God they weren't home to see what was happening.

Zachary pushed open the gate, and still hanging onto Truesdale's arm, he followed him into the yard. Truesdale leaned down and grabbed the dog's collar. "I'll have to take him around back."

Truesdale, both hands holding the collar of the huge black and brown dog, headed around the side of the house, Zachary alongside, fingers grasping the suspect's elbow.

Stacey, Lt. Stafford, Strickland and Abel Navarro approached the front entrance by way of a brick walk that curved through a thick, dichondra lawn. Before they reached the massive wood door, Zachary shouted, "Come back here, you bastard." Loud barks from Terminator punctuated his words.

"What the..." Stafford broke into a run, following the noise. Abel and Stacey dashed right behind him.

"I'll cover the front," Strickland said.

What happened was obvious as soon as they entered the back yard. Terminator was still loose but obviously thought he was part of a game. His stubby tail wagged and he continued to bark as he skidded across a redwood patio toward an open French door as Zachary's leg disappeared inside.

They heard him shout, "Halt," along with the pounding of running feet. Stafford galloped past the dog who stood poised by the open door. He looked expectantly toward Stacey and Abel as though awaiting an invitation to enter. Stacey was glad to see his tail wagging.

"Good dog." She gave him a quick pat on the head as she darted past.

The door opened into a high-ceilinged room with massive beams. Navajo rugs were scattered over a highly polished brown tile floor. Couches and chairs of white, chocolate, and tan leather faced the windowed wall sharing its view of the backyard and the sea beyond.

Shouts and pounding came from the direction of a long, wide hallway decorated with southwestern prints and paintings. Felix beat on the door. "Open the door, Truesdale."

"What happened?" Stafford asked.

"Suspect is stronger than he looks. Soon as we got out of sight, he jerked away from me and hightailed it inside. He was only five feet ahead, but he managed to get in there and lock the door." Felix banged his shoulder against the door, but it didn't give.

"Damn. He's probably going to destroy that book of his," Stafford said.

Strickland joined the others who were gathered

around the locked door. "What's going on?"

"I wasn't expecting him to bolt. He got away. Now he's locked himself in." Felix shook his head.

"We ought to be able to break the door down without too much trouble," Strickland said.

"It's pretty sturdy. Solid core." It was obvious Felix was miserable because the suspect got away from him.

Before they could decide what to do next, a loud blast echoed from inside.

Chapter 10

"He's got a gun," Stafford said unnecessarily. "Move away from the door, everyone. Strickland, notify the Chief that our suspect has a weapon."

Strickland backed several feet down the hallway to make the call on his cell phone.

Everyone stood silently, listening for any sound coming from the other side of the door. They heard nothing.

"Hey, Mr. Truesdale," Stafford shouted. "What's going on? Unlock the door and let us in."

There was no response.

"Please, open up."

Still nothing.

"You don't want us to break down this door, now do you?"

No answer.

"Come on, Mr. Truesdale."

Nothing.

Finally Stacey said," I think he shot himself."

"Me too," Abel agreed.

"Let's go in." Stafford lifted his heavily booted foot and aimed it under the doorknob while at the same time, Zachary banged against it with his shoulder. The lock gave way, and the door burst inward.

With guns drawn, Stafford and Zachary peered inside. All Stacey could see was white carpeting, the corner of a white satin covered bed, and a door slightly ajar leading into what was probably a bathroom.

"I can't see the suspect." Stafford said. "Watch yourselves." Holding their revolvers with both hands, Stafford moved inside to the left, Zachary to the right.

Abel covered them from behind. Stacey peeked around the doorjamb without entering.

After a few moments Stafford said, "It's all over. He's in the bathroom. Stay out, Stacey. You don't have to see this."

The warning came too late. Stacey had already stepped far enough inside the bedroom to see that Evan Truesdale had sat on the toilet seat, put the barrel of a .357 Magnum revolver in his mouth and fired. Blood and brain matter were spattered all over the walls, the toilet tank, the white tile of the counter, and the mirror. He was still on the toilet, but his upper body and what was left of his head rested against and all over the counter top. Stacey gasped and turned her head away. She fought the urge to vomit.

Felix said, "What a mess."

A drawer on one of the night stands hung open. It was easy enough to figure out that after Truesdale locked the door, he'd gone to the night stand for his gun, went into the bathroom and blew his brains out.

Zachary stood with his head down. "I'm sorry I let him get away from me."

Stacey put her hand on his shoulder. "Probably worked out better this way. He can't ever hurt another little girl."

Her words didn't seem to comfort him as he shook his head sadly.

"Stacey's right, you know," Abel said. "This is the perfect ending. These guys can't be cured. They do the time, get out, and they're right back at it."

"I'll call the coroner and the sheriff's department. They'll handle this part of the investigation. We need to search the house and find out where he stashed the book, but we're not going to be able to do anything like that until the crime scene guys are done. But we better notify the family, we sure don't want them walking in on this big mess without any warning. Wilbur, will you handle that? One of you guys, get the camera. We can start taking pictures."

"Sure."

As she took off to look for an appointment book or list of phone numbers, she heard Sergeant Stafford say, "Zachary, go outside and stand guard, keep anyone away who doesn't need to be here. Strickland, call the Chief and let him know the status here."

Abel stared at Truesdale's lifeless body and the blood spattered everywhere. He remembered Maria's admonishment about "suspended particles." Too late to worry about that now.

* * *

The ritual ended and the mourners scattered as they returned to their vehicles. Pastor Love and Reverend Cookmeyer embraced before striding across the marker-and-headstone-studded grass. With her head held high, Mrs. Danfelt marched a few feet ahead of Sally Jo Roberts and Hannah Love.

"Why don't we inject a little fear into Mrs. Love?" Frank suggested, as he draped an arm over an angel-topped monument. "Soften her up a bit for Wilbur."

Doug shrugged.

They moved quickly to intercept Mrs. Love. The choir director and the preacher's wife were engrossed in conversation, neither one noticed the approaching detectives.

"Excuse me," Frank said, reaching out and touching Mrs. Love's arm.

Sally Jo Roberts squealed, her mouth and eyes opened wide. "For goodness sake, where did you come from?"

Hannah Love frowned and absently rubbed the place Marshall touched.

"If you don't mind, we'd like to speak with Mrs. Love privately," Frank said.

"Well, yes, of course." Sally Jo looked and sounded relieved. "I'll just go tell your husband."

"We'll only be a moment," Doug said.

"What is it?" Hannah asked. She blinked several times, her eyes moving quickly from Doug to Frank.

"Got a couple of questions for you," Frank began.

"About what?" A lock of red hair blew across her face.

"Mallory Cookmeyer's murder."

Beneath the dusting of freckles on her cheeks, her pale skin flamed. "I only know what I've read in the papers and heard on television."

"We understand you spoke with Officer Wilbur," Doug said.

"And that you told her you were jealous of Mrs. Cookmeyer," Frank added. "What was that all about?"

"It was silly of me, really. But Mallory Cookmeyer was so beautiful and I knew my husband was counseling her. That's all there was to it."

"You sure there wasn't something that your husband did that made you feel that way? Usually where there's smoke, there's fire," Frank said.

"Absolutely not," she said a tad too loudly, and she no longer looked at either one of them.

Doug raised an eyebrow in Frank's direction. "We'd like to have Officer Wilbur have another chat with you."

"What on earth for? I answered all her questions. And really, I don't know anything that could be the least bit helpful." She took a tentative step in the direction where the rest of her party waited near the limousine.

"Oh, I have a hunch you'll think of something else," Frank said, smiling. "You're free to go now. Officer Wilbur will be in touch with you."

Mrs. Love nearly ran toward her waiting husband. He separated himself from the others and walked toward her. She threw herself into his arms. He scowled over her head in the direction of the detectives.

"I have no idea what it is, but that woman knows more than she's telling," Frank said. "I really don't think it'll take much for her to open up. Whatever she's concealing is eating at her."

"Soon as I can get hold of Stacey, I'll tell her to go after Mrs. Love." Doug wondered what Stacey was doing and if she was okay.

Chapter 11

Realizing her present apparel wasn't appropriate for talking to a new widow, before Stacey called the school, she called home.

"Mom, this is Stacey. I need you to do something for me as quickly as possible." She told her mother what clothes to put together and then spoke to her father, giving him directions to the Truesdale's home, instructing him about the urgency of him arriving quickly.

Stacey located Dorothy Truesdale at the grammar school where she worked as a teacher. After Stacey quickly explained to the shocked principal about Mr. Truesdale's death, Mrs. Truesdale was brought to the telephone. Stacey broke the news as gently as possible. Not surprisingly, the new widow expressed disbelief and horror. Arrangements were made to bring her home.

Fortunately the school was on the outskirts of

town giving Stacey enough time to wash the garish make-up from her face and rearrange her hair into a simpler do. Her father arrived with the clothes she'd requested, and though he glanced around curiously, he didn't ask any questions.

The coroner and the men from the sheriff's department crime scene team had arrived. The bedroom had been unsuccessfully searched and the Sgt. Stafford and the others were going through the BMW the tow truck had parked in the driveway.

By the time Mrs. Truesdale had been delivered to her house, Stacey was more appropriately dressed in neat slacks and a plain shirt, flats replacing the high-heels. Stacey stood in the front door to greet the pretty woman whose shock and disbelief about her husband's death was apparent in her expression.

In her mid-thirties, Dorothy Truesdale's pale blonde pageboy curled around her plump cheeks. Her slightly over-weight body was neatly clothed in a light blue striped jacket and skirt, with a darker blue tee-shirt. On her feet were white sneakers. She turned to stare at the men going through the BMW. "I don't understand...what are they doing to my husband's car?"

Stacey took Mrs. Truesdale's arm. "I'm so sorry for your loss, ma'am. I think you should come inside and sit down."

Tears threatened to spill from the woman's eyes. "This is all so terrible. I don't understand what's happened here."

One of the crime scene investigators bustled past, hurrying from the house. Mrs. Truesdale stared open mouthed at the lettering on his jacket, Ventura County Sheriff's Department, Crime Scene Investigator.

"Why don't we go into the kitchen where we'll be out of the way." Stacey led Mrs. Truesdale into the kitchen.

In the kitchen, Mrs. Truesdale glanced around, seeming to take control of herself. "I'll make some coffee."

"You don't have to do that. You need to sit down and let me explain a few things to you." Stacey said.

"I could use some coffee and I'm sure some of these men who are doing goodness knows what around here could too." Mrs. Truesdale put a pot of coffee together. She opened a cupboard and reached for a cup. It slipped from her fingers and shattered on the red tile counter top. She began to sob.

Stacey put her arm around Mrs. Truesdale and led her to a chair at the long, white table with red tile inserts that matched the counters. By the time Stacey had swept up the broken pottery the coffee was done. She poured a cup for Mrs. Truesdale and set it in front of her.

After wiping her eyes and blowing her nose, Mrs. Truesdale said, "I'm having a hard time understanding all this. If my husband committed suicide what are all these people doing here? Exactly what is going on?"

"What I'm going to tell you is going to be very difficult. Did you have any inclination, even a hint, that your husband had a problem?"

"What kind of problem? We've only lived here for a short while, not quite two years. He's already done a lot for the community. He is...was a very civic-minded man. He belongs to the Rocky Bluff Chamber of Commerce and the Rotary Club. We're members of the country club. We've made so many wonderful friends. He golfs with the city leaders and business men. This will be a shock to everyone."

"Mrs. Truesdale, there is no easy way to tell you this. Your husband was involved in something very bad–something to do with young girls."

Mrs. Truesdale shook her head. "No, I don't believe it."

"I'm so sorry to have to tell you all this. We're looking for a book of photographs. Have you ever seen anything like that? Pictures of your husband with young girls," Stacey asked.

Tears flooded Mrs. Truesdale's eyes. She shook her head. "Of course not. How can you even suggest such a thing. Evan would never do anything like that. He was the perfect husband...and the perfect father. This has to be a dreadful mistake."

"For your sake, I wish it was a mistake. But, I'm afraid it's all true."

Mrs. Truesdale turned in her chair and gazed through the large window facing the sea. When she turned back, she said, "There was something I remember Evan told me before we were married. Something his first wife accused him of... the reason why she divorced him. I remember it was about his daughter. But he didn't tell me the details and I never asked. His first wife was an alcoholic. No one believed her accusations."

"Do you know his first wife's name?"

"Of course, but I have no idea where you could find her. The last time we heard anything from her she was living in Orange County."

"What about his daughter? Did he keep in touch with her?"

She shook her head. "No. They didn't get along." Again tears brimmed and threatened to overflow. "He did pay child support though, until she turned eighteen."

Stacey pulled a notebook from her pocket. "Can you tell me their names and anything you know that might help us locate them."

Mrs. Truesdale pulled an address book from a drawer of the built-in desk, and dug through it. As she read names and phone numbers, Stacey copied them down.

After doing that, Mrs. Truesdale collapsed in her chair, gasping. "How am I going to tell Dennis and Casey about their father?"

"Your sons?"

"Yes. They will be absolutely devastated. They loved Evan so much."

"How old are they?"

"Dennis is six and Casey, four." The tears that had been threatening, cascaded down her cheeks.

"They're so young, Mrs. Truesdale. It will be difficult, of course."

"Oh, dear God, how will I ever explain all this?"

"They don't need to know everything."

"How can they help but not know. Surely it will be all over the papers and in the news. Everyone will be talking."

"No. We'll do our best to keep the circumstances surrounding your husband's death quiet. But about your kids, Mrs. Truesdale, what kind of arrangements are you going to make for them? Do they come home on a bus? They probably shouldn't come here."

"I'll call someone to pick Dennis up at school and Casey from day care. We'll stay at a friend's for awhile. How long is this going to take?"

"The coroner will be able to take the body away soon. They'll probably finish with this part of the investigation today or tomorrow." Stacey remembered the bloody scene where Mr. Truesdale had taken ended his life. "I hate to mention it, but the bathroom is a mess. It's not something you'll want to come home to."

Mrs. Truesdale shuddered.

"I'll give you the names of a couple of places in the county who will come in and clean it for you."

"Thank you, I'd appreciate that."

"I'll have to know where you'll be staying." Again Stacey wrote the information in the notebook.

"Should I start making plans for my children?"

"Yes, of course. But if you think of anything else I should know, be sure and tell me."

Stacey remained nearby while Dorothy Truesdale used the phone. She broke down several times while attempting to explain what had happened to her husband. Once Stacey had to take the phone and finish for her.

Once the phone calls were done, Mrs. Truesdale said, "I'll need to pack a few things for myself and the boys."

"You won't be able to go into your bedroom until

the men are through. Maybe you can borrow a few things for tonight. You'll probably be able to come back later this evening or in the morning. You can call the police station later on."

While Mrs. Truesdale was still in the kitchen, the body was removed. Stafford and Abel came back inside. Stacey stepped into the living room, and asked, "Did you find it?"

Sergeant Stafford shook his head. "We looked every place we could think of. It just isn't there. It's like he knew we were on to him and stashed it someplace safe."

"It's important for us to locate it. Even though the Truesdales haven't lived here too long, he has a lot of friends with influence in this community. Unless we have some real proof, we may run into a public relations problem," Stacey said.

"What about the wife?" Stafford motioned with his head toward the kitchen. "Did she know anything about her husband's nasty hobby?"

"No, but there was a hint of something in his past. Seems his first wife accused him of some sort of wrongdoing with his daughter. She may have been his first victim. We ought to be able to track her down. By the way, Mrs. Truesdale made a pot of coffee. And as soon as possible, someone needs to take her to be with her boys."

"I'll see to it." Stafford started for the kitchen.

"Would you mind if I took a turn looking for that book?" Stacey called after him.

"Be my guest."

Stacey remembered that her husband was never as good at finding things as she was. She grinned, wondering if that was a sexist thought. Whatever, it wouldn't hurt for a fresh eye to examine Truesdale's car.

While she searched, a police unit came and took Mrs. Truesdale away, and the rest of the team had a coffee break.

She began with the interior of the Mercedes,

methodically searching in all the obvious places, knowing full well that the other officers had been there before. Though she didn't unscrew the door panels, positive that was something the men had done, she peeked and poked in every other conceivable pocket and space.

The trunk was open, and as she started toward the back of the shiny, gold-colored vehicle, a thought tickled her memory. When she was a teenager, she'd gone through a brief rebellious period when she'd taken up smoking. She'd owned a convertible at the time and she kept the packs hidden in the place where the convertible top folded into the car. Perhaps Evan Truesdale had the same idea.

From the outside, there was no opening. But when she climbed in the back, she knelt on the smooth leather seats. Sliding her hand down, fingers extended, in the space created to receive the convertible top, she moved it slowly along until she made contact with something.

* * *

After a quick lunch, Frank and Doug returned to their office to review what they had learned.

"I think we should lean more on the secretary. I have a hunch she's the key to this whole thing. She either committed the murder, or she's hiding something that would open everything up for us." Frank popped a stick of gun in his mouth before settling himself at his desk.

Doug had his notebook opened and flipped through the pages. "Which means you think Cookmeyer may have killed his wife, with the assistance of his secretary."

"Yeah...I like them."

"What about motive?"

"In the secretary's case, to protect her boss. If it

was him, he wanted his wife out of the way so he could marry the cute little choir director."

"But she says they weren't having an affair."

"Sure."

"Okay, then what about her as the killer? Getting rid of her lover's wife is a great motive. She doesn't seem to have much of an alibi either."

Frank shook his head slowly and chomped on his gum. "Naw, I don't think so. She doesn't look the type to me."

Doug laughed. "I can't believe you said that. Since when is there a type to a murderer?"

"I know." Frank polished his bald head with his hand. "But she doesn't feel right to me."

"We don't want to forget Hannah Love. Jealousy can be a powerful reason to do something irrational."

"Yep. I'll be anxious to hear what else Stacey can get out of her."

"After all, dear Katherine Danfelt suggested Mallory might have been having an affair with Pastor Love. If that was so, and his wife knew it...well, there you are."

"Heard anything from your inquiry to L.A.P.D. about Pastor Love's tour on their force?"

"Not yet. What about that computer guy? The stalker. We gonna do anymore with him?"

"Naw, I don't see any reason to. His alibi is pretty tight. So what's our next move?"

"Let's take on the preacher and his secretary again. Whatever shindig they were having after the funeral ought to be about over now. I bet we can find them both at the church." Frank stood and grabbed his suit jacket off the arm of the chair.

"I hope Stacey is back by the time we're through. I think it's important that she talk to Mrs. Love today." Doug shrugged into his jacket as he followed his partner down the hall.

Chapter 12

"I've got it," Stacey announced, as she entered the kitchen, holding a small photograph album in her gloved hand. From their places around the tile-topped table, Strickland, Navarro, Zachary, and Stafford stared at her with various expressions on their faces, ranging from surprise to disbelief.

"Where'd you find it?" Navarro asked, straight black eyebrows raised.

"Not in the Mercedes," Stafford said.

"Yep, sure did." Stacey dropped the book on the table.

"How about that." Stafford sounded amazed. "Good work, Wilbur."

Zachary shook his head. "I can't believe it. I thought we searched everywhere."

"So where was it?" Strickland asked.

"Same place I used to hide my cigarettes when I

was seventeen." Stacey grinned. "In the space where the convertible top goes. I'll bet he never put the top down."

Sgt. Stafford flipped through the pages of the book. "Disgusting as this is, it's exactly what we needed. Truesdale is quite recognizable in every photo. They are quite explicit. The little girl is about eight years old."

Stacey felt sick to her stomach. She was glad Mrs. Truesdale was gone and didn't have to hear any of this.

"At least we've got what we needed to know there's no doubt about what that sick-o was up to," Stafford said. "Let's head back to the station."

The sheriff's team had finished with their investigation, packed up their equipment and left, with the Rocky Bluff team following them out the door.

On their way out to the van, Stacey stepped alongside Strickland. "Ryan, do you supposed you could keep this dark side of Mr. Truesdale quiet? His kids don't need to be hurt any more than they already will be by their father's death."

Ryan nodded. "I have to let the press know it was a suicide though, I don't think there's anyway to squelch that information. But I'll do my best about the other."

"Thanks."

When they were back in the van and about to leave, Felix said, "I just wish I hadn't moved those cuffs."

Abel reached up to momentarily clasp Felix's muscular shoulder. "Quit worrying about it, man. The guy's dead. It's for the best."

"It isn't over," Stacey said.

"All that's left is documenting and storing the evidence and filing our reports." Stafford started the van.

"There's that, but even more important is locating Truesdale's daughter, making sure she gets some counseling, if she hasn't already." Stacey had taken down the names and addresses. She hoped Chief McKenzie would let her do the follow up.

* * *

Stacey climbed from the van just as Doug and Frank came out the back door. Doug waved and trotted toward her. With amusement apparent in his expression, he said, "Darn, I was hoping you'd still be wearing your skimpy little get-up."

She felt her face flush. "Hopefully you won't ever see me like that."

"I bet you looked pretty sexy. I'd like to have seen you."

"Well, I'm gad you didn't." She was embarrassed by his comments even though she knew he was only teasing.

His tone changed. "I need you to do something for me today."

"I'm going to a debriefing with the chief now. I don't know how long that will take. I have to write my report and there's something I need to follow up on. What is it you want me to do?"

"I'd like you to interview Hannah Love again. I'd really appreciate it if you could squeeze it in." Doug's blue eyes pleaded along with his words.

"I'll try, okay?"

"Okay. Maybe we can get together later and compare notes. I'm really curious about what you were up to in that cute little outfit of yours."

"Hey. Wilbur," Strickland hollered from the yawning door into the department. "You don't want to keep the Chief waiting too long."

* * *

Stacey joined the de-briefing, filling the Chief in on what happened between the time she turned the wire off and back on again, and giving her view of the arrest and Evan Truesdale's escape and suicide.

Felix Zachary bemoaned the fact that he was the one to move the handcuffs making the escape and suicide possible, and once again he was reassured that it was a satisfactory ending to the crime.

"Yeah, Felix," Abel interjected, "Think of all the money you saved the taxpayers."

"And the grief you saved the family if it had come to trial," Stacey said.

The Chief outlined what information Strickland should give to the press, admonished the group not to discuss the details of the case with family members and friends outside the department, before sending everyone off to write their reports.

Stacey started to get up, but the Chief said, "I have something else to talk to you about, Officer Wilbur."

"Yes, sir." She expected to be told not to help Doug.

Chief McKenzie took off his glasses and polished them. "As you know, the department is in the process of hiring more officers."

Stacey nodded, wondering what that had to do with her.

"I'd like to upgrade you, and give you the job of Vice Detective. Will you consider it?"

Shocked by his offer, Stacey didn't know what to say. She'd never considered working in vice. Her recent experience hadn't exactly been pleasant. However, she certainly felt satisfaction from knowing Truesdale would never again harm a little girl. There were other men and women like Truesdale who committed deviant crimes on children. But if she took the job it would probably make it even harder for her and Doug to see each other.

"Sir, could I have some time to think about this?"

"Of course, but don't take too long. I'm anxious to get this organized. We'll be starting small, just you and one other officer. It means a raise in pay, of course."

"Yes, sir, I understand. But I'd like to discuss it with my family."

"Let me know by the end of the week."

"Yes, sir. There's something else I wanted to talk

to you about."

He looked surprised.

"I'd like permission to follow up on Truesdale's daughter from his former marriage."

"We don't need anymore evidence."

"I know, sir. Since he didn't have a record, he obviously wasn't prosecuted for molesting her. It might help her to know what's happened, and if she hasn't had any counseling, she ought to get some."

Chief McKenzie beamed. "I knew my instincts were right. You have exactly the compassion needed to head up this unit."

It was Stacey's turn to be surprised. Head up the unit? She would be the one in charge? Wow.

"Let the watch commander know what kind of hours you'll be working to finish this. We'll talk some more when you give me your decision. As one of your first assignments, I'd like you to see if you can find out the identify of the victim pictured in Truesdale's album."

It sounded like he expected her to say "yes." Well, why wouldn't he? It was an increase in pay and a promotion, along with a great deal of responsibility. Not bad for a female officer.

"Thanks, Chief."

Her next task was to find an empty desk and a telephone.

＊ ＊ ＊

Ryan Strickland organized his notes and put together a simple statement to the press announcing Evan Truesdale's death by his own hand, and that he left no note. Evidently neither the newspapers or other media felt Truesdale was prominent enough to question him further. If word leaked about the reason for his suicide, that would be another matter.

The minute Ryan entered his home that

afternoon, Barbara greeted him. "What's the deal with Evan Truesdale? What happened to him? Did he really commit suicide? Why on earth for? He lived in that gorgeous house on the bluffs. He had two nice little boys."

Ryan held up his hands and shook his head. "There's not much I can tell you about this one. Aren't you going to kiss me hello?"

"I'm sorry." She threw her arms. around him, and kissed him soundly. "You have no idea how crazy it's been around here. The phone keeps ringing. The school secretary was first. She's the one who told me Mrs. Truesdale had been called home because her husband committed suicide."

"Let's go to the kitchen. I could use a good cup of coffee. This has been a really hectic day."

"Of course, sweetheart. I've got a pot on already. Honestly, I've hardly been able to get anything done." She set a mug of delicious smelling brew in front of him, continuing her monologue until she sat beside him. "Those darling boys...we've seen them on the soccer field...and Mrs. Truesdale, she's Tony's teacher. He's sure going to be full of questions. Okay, now, what's going on?" She put her chin in her hand and stared expectantly at him.

At that moment, Ryan decided to go against his own advice and that of the Chief's. He knew he could trust Barbara.

"You must not breathe to another living soul what I'm going to tell you."

"Of course I won't say anything." Her eyes rounded.

"Evan Truesdale killed himself because he was a pedophile and we found out about him. We have the evidence to prove it."

Barbara's mouth opened, but she didn't say anything.

"It'll be a lot better for the family if none of this gets out."

"It's so hard to believe. I met Evan a couple of times. He seemed like a perfectly normal and quite charming man. Did his wife know?"

"Not until we told her what we knew about him and his despicable hobby. It was hard for her to accept."

"Oh, dear, poor thing. She must be absolutely destroyed." She thought for awhile. "What can I tell people?"

"Exactly what I put in my press release and no more. Yes, he was a suicide and that he didn't leave a note."

"Okay, that's what I'll do."

* * *

Stacey was just leaving the station when she ran into Doug and Frank returning. "Hey, just the gal I want to see," Doug said.

"Wilbur, heard you were on special assignment? How'd it go?" Frank asked.

"Worked out okay."

"Good. See you inside, Milligan." Frank winked at Doug before disappearing through the door.

"Have you set up a meeting with Hannah Love yet?" Doug asked.

"As a matter of fact, I have."

"Good. Can we get together later, maybe over dinner."

"Not dinner. I haven't seen Davey all day. I want to eat with him."

"Sure. How about coffee at my place then? Hopefully Gordon will work his entire shift tonight. I've got lots to tell you about this murder case. I'd like to hear about your undercover operation."

"I'll be there after I get Davey settled for the night. By the way, when you see Gordon, ask him what the heck he was doing in the old part of town this morning. He darn near ruined the whole operation."

Chapter 13

Hannah Love sounded even less enthusiastic about meeting with Stacey the second time than she'd been the first. Still wearing her street clothes and driving her VW bug, Stacey hoped Mrs. Love would be forthright in her answers.

Dressed in jeans and a light-green sweatshirt, her curly red hair tied back with a blue-and-white polka dotted bandana, Hannah opened the front door and stepped out on the porch. She watched Stacey climb from her car, walk down the cement path that bisected the neat lawn, and up the front steps.

"Hello," Hannah greeted, without smiling. "Like I said on the phone, I already told you everything I know. This is really a waste of time for both of us. I'm trying to get my house in order for a women's Bible study I'm having later."

"This won't take long. The detectives in charge of

investigating Mallory Cookmeyer's murder thought it would be a good idea if we talked again, in case there was something you might have forgotten."

"I've gone over everything in my mind, and truly I can't think of anything at all that could possibly help. If you really think it's necessary, I suppose you should come in." She stepped aside reluctantly, allowing Stacey to enter

Hannah didn't offer her a seat, nor did she take one. Instead she stood with her arms. crossed and her legs slightly apart. "What exactly do you want to know?"

"Tell me more about your husband's counseling. What kind of people use his services?"

Hannah rolled her eyes indicating she couldn't understand the significance of the question. "People who have problems, of course. Usually members of our congregation."

"Aren't some of these people women?"

"Of course. The majority are. What difference does that make?"

"Do you get jealous every time your husband counsels a female member of your congregation?"

She glared at Stacey." Of course not."

"What I'm trying to find out, Mrs. Love, is what made you jealous when he counseled Mallory Cookmeyer?"

"I never should have told you that." Hannah turned her back on Stacey.

"But you did, and now I'd like to understand what was behind that jealousy."

It was several minutes before Hannah faced Stacey again. When she did her eyes were filled with tears. "Did you know Mallory Cookmeyer? She was everything I'm not. Beautiful and sophisticated, and she always wore such gorgeous clothes. Look at me, I'm a plain Jane by comparison. What man wouldn't be attracted to her."

"But she was married."

"Her marriage wasn't happy. Everyone knew that.

Of course Joshua never told me, but I suspected that was why she turned to him for counseling."

"What about your marriage? How would you classify it?"

"About as good as anyone else's. At least it seemed to be until Mallory started taking up so much of Joshua's time. Not only did she have regular sessions with him at the church, sometimes they met other places. She even called him here."

"As you told me, counseling troubled people is part of what your husband does. Do you have any proof he was being unfaithful to you?"

"No proof, I felt it here." She clenched her fist to the center of her chest.

"Has he ever been unfaithful to you in the past?"

Mrs. Love's face puckered. Huge tears spilled down her face. "Yes."

Stacey put her arm around the sobbing woman and guided her toward a large, dark blue arm chair. "Why don't you sit down, and tell me about it?"

When Mrs. Love was able to control herself, she explained, "Joshua only strayed once before. It was while he was still a police officer and before he became a Christian. You have no idea how painful that was. I really thought that sort of thing was all behind us. Then I began to notice the same tell-tale signs as before. He was distracted all the time, like his mind was elsewhere. And he was gone so much."

"Not to defend your husband, but doesn't Pastor Love's profession require him to be away from home a lot?"

"Yes, but he used to share with me what he was doing, but for the last few months he has hardly discussed anything with me."

From the dining room, a deep, sonorous voice boomed, "Oh, my poor darling." Pastor Joshua Love strode into the room and sat on the arm of the chair, clasping his wife's hand possessively.

Mrs. Love gasped, "Oh, Joshua, how long have you

been listening?"

"Long enough to know I've been neglecting my wife. I'm certainly going to have to make up for it." He smoothed red tendrils away and kissed her forehead. "Let me assure you, dearest Hannah, no matter how it may have looked to you, Mallory Cookmeyer and I were not having an affair. I wish you'd told me how you were feeling before this."

He tipped her chin upward, and moved his lips to hers. Before he made contact, Mrs. Love pulled away. Pastor Love stared at his wife, his lower lip pushed out in an unmistakable pout.

After a few embarrassing moments, Stacey cleared her throat.

"Sorry you had to witness this private moment, " Pastor Love said, standing. He put out his hand, grasped Stacey's firmly and shook it. "Joshua Love. I don't think we've met."

"Officer Wilbur, Rocky Bluff P.D."

"If you don't have more business with my wife, it seems we really need some time alone." He smiled at Stacey.

She shook her head "I'd like to finish so I don't have to come back."

Still smiling, he perched again on the chair arm. "Fine, but please be brief."

"Mrs. Love, what were you doing Saturday evening from around nine until eleven?"

"I went to a movie," she said quickly.

"Who did you go with?"

Mrs. Love glanced down at her hands in her lap. "No one. I went by myself."

"Is that usual for you to go to a movie alone at such a late hour?"

Mrs. Love glanced at her husband before answering. "It was a movie I'd been wanting to see for quite some time."

"What was the name of it and where was it playing?" Stacey asked.

Shrugging, Mrs. Love said, "The Palace Theater. I can't remember the name of the movie. But it's the one everyone's talking about. Tom Cruise's latest."

"Is that all?" Pastor Love asked.

"Not quite. I may as well ask, where were you during that same time period, sir?"

"Meditating and going over my sermon like I do most Saturday evenings," the preacher said. "To answer the question I know you'll be asking next, no, there isn't anyone who can verify that. I was working in my study at the church. The most I can hope for is that someone may have seen my light on."

"What time did you finish?" Stacey asked.

"I have no idea. Time has a way of getting away from me when I'm working like that."

"Was your wife here when you got home that night?"

He hesitated and frowned. "Ah...why, yes, I'm sure she was. Of course. Anything else?"

His hesitation made Stacey wonder if his answer was truthful.

Though she hadn't found out anything concrete, the interview had stirred up more uncertainties. She wondered what Doug would make of it. Since she couldn't think of anything else to ask, she said, "No, that's all."

He stood. "I'll see you to your car." Before walking after Stacey, he leaned down and kissed Mrs. Love again. "I'll be right back, sweetheart."

Stacey hesitated at the bottom of the stairs. "There are a couple of questions I'd like to ask you. How long did you counsel Mrs. Cookmeyer?"

He thought for a moment, tucking his shirt into the waistband of his slacks. Though stocky, Pastor Love wasn't fat, there was no flab above his belt. "I'd have to consult my calendar to tell you exactly, but two or three months, maybe."

"Were you counseling Mrs. Cookmeyer about her marriage?"

"As you know, Officer Wilbur, even though Mallory is deceased, what went on during her counseling sessions is still protected by the laws of confidentiality. But I can tell you the reason she came to me was because she was having trouble with a male member of her church and her husband didn't take it seriously. She wanted to know how to handle the whole situation without offending the man."

"It doesn't seem like it would take two or three months to come up with a way to end unwanted attention," Stacey said.

"Without imparting any privileged information, I believe it would be safe to say that Mallory found me a good listener, and I soon learned that she had more serious problems than she revealed at first. That is as much as I feel comfortable telling you about Mallory Cookmeyer. Have a good evening, Officer Wilbur." After aiming another smile at Stacey, he bounded back up the stairs and vanished inside his house.

Stacey wished she knew what secrets Mallory Cookmeyer revealed to Pastor Love.

* * *

A rich garlic and basil scent greeted Stacey when she opened the front door of the house.

"Mommy, Mommy," Davey called, and threw himself at her, squeezing her around the waist. "You're home."

She scooped him up and gave him a huge hug. "How's my boy?"

"I made a new friend at school. His name's Scotty. We played with the big blocks. Grandpa took me to the park."

"He did?"

"Yep. He pushed me on the swings and I went down the big slide all by myself."

"Wow."

Clara peered out from the kitchen. "Dinner's almost ready."

"It's s'ghetti," Davey said.

Stacey put him down. "Yum. I can hardly wait." She realized she hadn't eaten lunch, and she was ravenous. "I'm going to take a quick shower and change."

"Hurry, dear." Clara said, "Dad and I are anxious to hear about your day."

The family was already around the table when Stacey joined them. She wore her favorite pale green sweater that hung comfortably over her denim clad hips.

Her mother passed her the bowl of pasta. "How did everything go, dear?"

"Quite well, actually. Unfortunately I can't tell you the details, but it all worked out."

"Did wearing that dreadful outfit help?" Clara asked, handing her the bowl of sauce.

"Yes, mom, it did." She began eating. "Ummm, this is wonderful. I'm famished."

"Have some garlic bread." Her father offered her the plate.

Her parents and Davey ate and made small talk while Stacey concentrated on her food. When she'd had enough, Stacey said, "I do have some news I wanted to run by you."

Clara and Clyde gazed at her expectantly.

"Chief McKenzie has offered me a job with a much better salary."

"How nice, dear," Clara said.

Clyde's eyes narrowed. "What kind of job?"

"Detective. In Vice. He said I'd head the team. Of course, there would only be one other person for awhile."

"Vice?" Clara frowned and turned toward her husband. "Would that mean you'd have to dress in those skimpy outfits all the time?"

"Maybe once in awhile, I don't know."

"Will it be dangerous?" Clara asked.

Her father frowned. "Yes, I'd like to know that too. I'm not comfortable with the thought that my daughter will be putting herself in jeopardy."

"I'm glad you're both so concerned, but I'm sure it won't be nearly as dangerous as being a street cop."

"It sounds like a promotion." Still frowning, Clyde said. "Does it mean more money?"

"It's definitely a promotion, and yes, it will be a bigger salary."

Clyde asked, "Are you going to do it?"

"I told him I'd think about it. I'm truly honored he thinks I can do the job, but my hours will be erratic."

"I think you ought to consider it, Stacey." Her father beamed at her proudly. "It'll be a real feather in your cap. Detective Wilbur. Sounds good."

"I am. But I might have to be away from Davey, even more than I am now."

Davey stopped eating, fork in midair. He frowned at his mother.

"We love taking care of him," Clara said.

Stacey leaned closer to her son. "There might be times we have something planned, and I'll have to work."

"Don't do it then. I don't like you being gone so much," Davey said.

"That's what I'm worried about. I don't like being away from you either." She leaned over and gave him a hug.

Clyde cleared his throat. "Davey, you know we've talked about this before. Your mother does something that really helps people. Now they want her do something that's even more important. Don't you think you've a big enough boy now that you can be away from your mother without being upset?"

Davey stared down at his lap for a moment. "Long as Grandma or Grandpa will be here to take care of me, I guess it'll be okay."

It wasn't as if he hadn't already experienced many

times his grandparents had to substitute for her.

Clara smiled brightly. "You know we will be. We'll keep on having lots of fun together like we always do."

That seemed to appease Davey. He attacked his spaghetti with renewed enthusiasm.

"I'll make my decision before tomorrow." Stacey wanted to run the whole idea by Doug first and get his reaction. "That brings up something else. You know I've been helping Detective Milligan with his investigation of Mallory Cookmeyer's murder."

"Sure," Clyde said. Clara poured them each another cup of coffee and refilled Davey's milk glass.

"Does the church own Reverend Cookmeyer's house?" she asked.

"Oh, heavens no," Clara said. "We do well financially, but not enough to buy a parsonage like that."

"Mallory bought that with part of her inheritance from her folks," Clyde added. "Paid cash."

"What kind of money are we talking about?" Stacey asked.

"Lots," Clyde said. "I don't know the exact figure, of course, but it's been rumored that it was more than two million."

"I suppose now it all belongs to Reverend Cookmeyer," Stacey commented, mainly to herself.

"That's the way it usually works in California. What belongs to the wife, belongs to the husband." Clyde stood and pushed his chair against the table. "Time for the news."

Stacey stood. "I hate to leave again, Davey, but there's somewhere I have to go." She rumpled his hair and kissed his cheek.

"'S okay. Grandpa bought me some new Legos today." He jumped down and ran out of the room.

"What is it now, dear? It does seem to me you've put in an awful lot of hours already today," Clara said.

"I really need to talk to Doug."

Clara smiled. "He's such a nice young man."

"Yes, he is. I appreciate you taking care of Davey

for me, Mom." She kissed her mother's soft, plump cheek.

✳ ✳ ✳

The sound of squeaky brakes signaled Gordon's arrival in his police unit at the house. He bounded inside, leather belt squeaking. "Hey, Doug, anything good to eat? I'm starved."

"There's stew in the crock pot. Help yourself." Doug was finishing his second helping.

While Gordon was in the kitchen dishing up his dinner, he said, "Hey, I ran into Stacey downtown this morning. She was all decked out like a prostitute. Looked pretty hot, actually."

Doug had to control himself to keep from saying something mean to Gordon. "Yeah, I saw her. She told me you came close to ruining an undercover operation. What the heck were you doing in that part of town anyway?"

"Hey, I got out of there as soon as she told me what was going on. If you must know, I was looking for a part for my car. There's a wrecking yard right around the corner from where Stacey was hanging out." He brought his full bowl to the table and sat down.

"I've got a favor to ask you," Doug said.

Gordon began eating. "Hey, this is good," he mumbled and chewed at the same time. "Got to hand it to you, man, you really know how to cook."

"Take your break somewhere else tonight, okay? Hit one of the local cafes." Doug carried his empty bowl into the kitchen. "I'm having company."

Gordon lifted his head and grinned. "Oh yeah? Couldn't be Stacey, by any chance?"

"It really isn't any of your business, but yeah, it's Stacey." Gordon could be so irritating at times. "We've got a lot to talk about, both business and personal. I'd appreciate it if I didn't have to worry about you barging in while she's here."

"Sure, man. Never let it be said that Gordon Butler got in the way of a budding romance."

Chapter 14

"Heard you worked a suicide today," Maria said. She'd bought Chinese take-out for dinner and was in the process of dishing it up when Abel arrived home after picking up Lupita at his mother's. Maria had changed from her uniform into jeans and a light green sweater that emphasized her curves.

"News sure gets around," Abel said.

"This is still a small town after all." Maria dumped the Moo Goo Gai Pan on a platter. "Wash your hands, Lupita. Time to eat."

Lupita ran down the hall toward the bathroom while Maria stood with her hands on her hips facing Abel. "So?"

Abel scooped a handful of crisp noodles from a bowl and started to eat them. "So, what?"

"What kind of a suicide was it?"

"What do you mean?"

"You know what. Pills, carbon monoxide, gun, knife, what?"

Abel laughed. His wife was definitely a fanatic. "The guy blew his brains out, and yes, there was blood all over. But I was a good boy. I put on my protective gear and I got everyone else to do the same."

"Good. And did you wash up afterwards?"

"Yes, ma'am." He opened his arms to her. "Come here, babe, I'm safe."

"Great." Maria snuggled against him and kissed him soundly.

* * *

After settling Stacey on the couch, Doug poured two cups of coffee, put them on the table and sat next to her. "You look fantastic."

She laughed. "Anything would be better than the way I was dressed this morning."

"Well...I don't know. Butler said you were pretty sexy." He wished he'd seen her, but he wasn't happy how many of the guys had been treated to the same view.

She ignored his remark. "Do you want to hear what I found out from Hannah Love?"

"Oh, you did get a chance to meet with her? Great."

"Not only Mrs. Love but Pastor Love too. Quite interesting, in fact." She related what had happened, taking sips of her coffee from time to time. She concluded with," You know it's too bad whoever makes the coffee at the station can't do as good a job as you. You make the best coffee I've ever tasted."

"Thanks. So what's your take on all that stuff about the Loves?" Doug asked.

"Unless she's a great actress, I think Mrs. Love was telling it like it was. She felt her husband was having an affair with Mallory Cookmeyer and it made her extremely unhappy. Unhappy enough for her to do something about it, I don't know. But neither she nor her husband have decent alibis. It'll be easy enough to check to see if that movie she claimed to be watching was playing at that time, maybe even if the ticket seller remembered her, which isn't likely. But just because she went into the show, doesn't mean she stayed there."

Doug grinned at her. "You're really getting good at this."

"I don't know about that. It all seems obvious. Merely because there was a light on in Pastor Love's study at the church doesn't mean he was actually there. He's got the same kind of lousy alibi as Reverend Cookmeyer."

"What about the good pastor?"

"He's smooth. I think he listened to the whole conversation with his wife. He could hardly wait to get me out of the house so he could placate her. It wouldn't hurt to lean on him more."

"I'll do that tomorrow. We certainly have no shortage of suspects. Frank thinks Mrs. Danfelt did it to protect her boss."

"Protect him from what?"

"Scandal. She's convinced something is going on between Cookmeyer and the choir director. With the wife out of the picture, the gossips won't be so interested in his shenanigans."

Stacey grinned. "You're wrong about that. Anything a minister does that has even a hint of sin is going to cause an uproar."

"Frank doesn't like Katherine Danfelt, and the feeling is mutual. He'd like to arrest her to pay her back for her meanness." He drank some more coffee. "We did find out one more interesting tidbit from her about her boss."

"What's that?"

"Seems the Reverend Cookmeyer is in some kind of difficulty with his personal finances."

"Really?"

"According to Mrs. Danfelt, he made some foolish investments, more than he could afford, and they've gone sour."

"Interesting. The preacher may have had an even greater reason for wanting his wife dead. Mallory's parents left her a couple of million. Now the house is his as well as whatever else she owned. Wouldn't be the first time money motivated someone to murder."

"Well, well. This case is getting more interesting all the time. We found out this afternoon that Pastor Love wasn't all that great a police officer. Frank's source at the LAPD was pretty close-mouthed about it, but it was obvious his department was glad to get rid of him."

"Was he fired or did he quit?" Stacey asked.

"Quit."

"Whatever it was they had against him couldn't be much or surely they would have fired him, don't you think?"

"Seems that way." Doug put his arm around Stacey's shoulder. He studied her profile. Her short hair was swept back from her face revealing her smooth brow, her straight nose, full lips and strong, determined chin. He wanted to pull her close and kiss her, but as he moved toward her, she turned away. Her serious expression stopped him.

"There's something important I need to discuss with you."

He frowned. "What's that?"

"Chief McKenzie offered me a job today."

"Oh, yeah? What?"

"Vice-detective."

All sorts of thoughts piled into his brain, one on top of the other. He wasn't sure how he felt about the news. "Are you going to have to wear those sleazy clothes all the time?"

Stacey laughed. "That's exactly what my mother asked."

"Will you take the job?"

"That's why I wanted to talk to you. I don't know.

It's more money. I'd be head of the team, though for now, there'll only be one other member."

"Do you know who that'll be?"

"No, the Chief didn't say."

"I don't suppose that matters. How do you feel about it?"

"It's quite an honor, I never thought I'd get a promotion this soon, if at all."

"I always hoped you'd end up in my unit."

Stacey reached out and caressed his cheek. "That would have been nice."

"We'll probably have a devil of a time trying to get together," Doug said.

"My thoughts exactly."

"I don't see how you can pass up this chance."

"Me either."

"You have to tell the Chief you'll take it."

"I'm glad you feel that way because that's what I've decided to do."

Obviously she'd made up her mind before she'd even broached the subject with him. She merely wanted his assurance to bolster her confidence. Her strong personality was a big part of what attracted him to her. "We'll have to make time to be together."

Stacey nodded.

Awkwardness settled upon him as he gazed at her. "It seems like we've been friends for a long time, yet I really don't know a whole lot about you."

"Same here."

He perceived that she was experiencing a similar discomfort; neither one knew quite how to proceed.

"You know my wife left me and took our kids." It wasn't a subject he enjoyed discussing.

"What was she like?"

"Kerrie? She was redheaded and beautiful. But she hated my job. When Al Bertalone was killed, that was more-or-less the end of our marriage."

"You loved her very much, didn't you?"

He nodded. "Yeah, I did. But looking back, I

realize she wasn't the woman I thought she was. Even if Al hadn't died, our marriage would not have survived with her hating my profession the way she did. Somewhere along the line, she would have found an excuse to end it."

"Police work is hard on marriages, but I don't have first hand knowledge. When I was first married, I worked as a dispatcher and I saw a lot of marriages fall apart. When Davey was born, I stayed home."

"What about your marriage? All I've heard is that your husband died."

She nodded. "The good memories are overshadowed by the pain that surrounded David's death. We certainly loved each other, and Davey is a product of that love. He looks a lot like his dad."

"At least if you and I married, law enforcement would never come between us," Doug said.

Stacey turned pink. "No, I guess it wouldn't. We'd always have something to talk about."

"That kind of sounded like a marriage proposal, didn't it?" Doug leaned closer to her.

"No, not really," Stacey said. "I understood what you meant."

"I meant it to be a marriage proposal."

She remained quiet.

"What's your answer, Stacey? Will you marry me?"

"Oh, Doug, I don't know. I care for you a lot, but I haven't thought about marriage. I had a rule not to date anyone who worked for Rocky Bluff P.D." She laughed. "When I met you, I forgot about my rule and hoped that someday you'd ask me out."

"I'm glad you decided to break it." He was so close to her that their lips nearly touched.

"Me too."

His mouth found hers and his arms tightened around her. She was a delightful combination of softness and strength. She tasted sweet and smelled faintly of cinnamon. Though the kiss was wonderful, and he loved holding Stacey close, he knew this was not the right time for them to make love. Stacey must have felt it too because she slowly pulled away and glanced at her watch.

"I should go. I've got a busy day tomorrow. Wouldn't want to mess up the first day on a new job."

"Think about it, Stacey. Give me an answer soon. Nothing would make me happier than having you for my wife."

Chapter 15

Stacey began her new job without fanfare. She was given a desk at the back of a big room with five other desks, used by various officers at different times. It afforded little privacy, but she had a telephone and computer. The Chief's single instruction was, "You'll be wearing civilian clothes now, but hang onto your uniforms. You may need them from time to time."

Since no one else was in the room, she asked, "Who is going to be working with me?"

Chief McKenzie's only comment was, "When you need help, let me know," and he left her alone. So much for another member of her team.

The dispatchers and other officers were told to report all vice crimes to her, but no one had. This gave her the time to follow up on Evan Truesdale's daughter, Evangeline. Yesterday she'd made some preliminary calls.

Using the numbers given to her by the second Mrs. Truesdale, Stacey had finally reached an answering machine for the first Mrs. Truesdale and left a message that hadn't been returned. She decided to try again.

This time it was answered by a low-throated, female voice. Obviously the person had been awakened by the call. Stacey glanced at her watch. It was quarter to nine.

"I'm Officer Wilbur from the Rocky Bluff Police Department. Is this Mrs. Karen Truesdale?"

"That was my name once. Now it's Nelson." The voice turned cold and snappy. "What is this about anyway? I've been divorced from Evan for years. I don't know anything about him."

"Yes, ma'am, but I have some news that you might be interested in."

"I can't imagine anything about him that would interest me."

"Evan Marshall died by his own hand yesterday."

After a moment of silence, Karen Nelson said, "Good, but I still don't know what that has to do with me."

"I'd like to get in touch with your daughter, Mrs. Nelson."

"Evie isn't going to care what happened to him. She hated Evan."

"Mrs. Nelson, was your daughter molested by Mr. Truesdale?"

"That's what she said, but no one believed her. At first, not even me. But I caught him with her in her bedroom. My God, she was only eight. I blew my fuse. Threw him out of the house. Even reported him to the cops, but they didn't do anything. Evan was a big time architect, pals with the D.A. and the police chief. He told them that I was trying to get back at him for leaving me. They bought it."

"Did she ever get any help?"

"What do you mean help? Just getting away from him was all the help she needed."

"I meant counseling."

"No, we didn't have money for anything like that. We had to get along on my wages and the little bit Evan sent for child support. It wasn't an easy life until I met my new husband."

"Mrs. Nelson, do you have a number where I could reach your daughter?"

"Oh, yeah, sure. She's at work right now, but she'd probably be glad to hear your news. Go ahead and call her. Ask for Evie Nelson, she hasn't been called Evangeline Truesdale since we left Evan."

Either Mrs. Nelson had recovered from her alcoholism, or she never had a problem. That was another part of the big lie Evan Truesdale passed on to his new wife.

Stacey dialed the number.

"Dr. Alpert's office," a sweet voice answered.

Stacey introduced herself before asking, "May I speak with Evie Nelson, please?"

"This is Evie."

"I'm Detective Stacey Wilbur and I'm calling to let you know that your father, Evan Truesdale, committed suicide yesterday."

There was a long silence followed by, "I really don't give a damn."

"Evie, we know that your father sexually molested you when you were a child."

The sounds of crying came from the other end of the phone.

"Are you all right?"

"Someone besides my mother finally believes me."

"Yes, ma'am, the entire Rocky Bluff Police Department knows what your father did to you. A terrible crime. I'm sorry no one believed you before."

"Me too," she sniffled. "But I don't understand why..."

"I think it's important for you to realize that there are others who know what happened to you. Evie, have you ever thought about getting some counseling?"

"Oh, I don't know. I don't like to think about what happened."

"No, but I bet you do anyway."

"Yes, ma'am, sometimes I can't help myself."

"There are people you can talk to who can help you with all this."

"Actually, I have thought about doing something like that but..."

"I'd like you to promise me that you'll talk to a professional and do it very soon. Okay?"

"I'll think about it. And thank you, thank you for calling and telling me that my father can't hurt anyone else."

"You're welcome, Evie."

Stacey hung up the phone and smiled. There was one more thing she needed to do to put closure on the Evan Truesdale case, and that was to try to find the identity of the child in the pictures in his album. It was too early to talk to any prostitutes to find out if any of them knew who the girl was. She couldn't sit there waiting for someone to give her a job.

Thinking about all this made her head ache. She needed to keep busy. Grabbing her purse, she headed for Doug's office. Maybe he had something she could do.

She thought about the night before and smiled. Doug's proposal pleased her, but she hadn't made a decision. She certainly cared for him, whether it was love or not, she wasn't sure. What she felt for him wasn't the same as her love for David. But maybe she wasn't allowing herself to love Doug, fearing the dreadful pain she'd experienced when she lost David.

She smiled. Certainly the sexual attraction was there.

If they continued to be alone together, eventually they'd make love. Goodness knew, they both wanted to, and it was bound to happen sooner or later. When it did, a further complication would be added to their relationship. Complication? She wondered why she used that word. Then she knew exactly why.

It was time her son had a father in his life. Granted, her own father had done a terrific job with Davey, but it wasn't the same. And that brought up another problem—her parents. What would they think about losing both her and Davey?

The phone was ringing when she knocked on Doug's office door. When it kept ringing, she realized no one was there. She dashed inside and snatched up the receiver from the nearest desk. "Detective Milligan's office."

There was a long pause, before a timid male voice said, "Is Detective Milligan there?"

"No, I'm sorry. This is Detective Wilbur. How can I help you?"

"My name is Louis Beltran."

Stacey remembered he was the computer guy who stalked Mallory Cookmeyer. "I'll be glad to give a message to Detective Milligan."

"I suppose that'll be okay." He paused a long while before continuing. "I wouldn't want you people to think any less of Mallory, because she truly was a wonderful woman, but I think Detective Milligan needs to know that she was seeing another man."

"By seeing another man, what do you mean exactly?" Stacey asked.

"That she was romantically involved with someone. It wasn't her fault, you see. Her husband neglected her. Any woman would have done the same. I just wish she had accepted what I offered. She might be alive today."

"Do you know the name of the other man?" Stacey asked.

"Of course. That's why I'm calling. Detective Milligan needs to investigate him."

"He most certainly will, just tell me the name."

"Joshua Love. He's the minister of All Saint's Calvary Church. You know that big brick..."

"Yes, I know the one. What makes you think Pastor Love and Mallory Cookmeyer were having an affair?"

"Well..." he paused, obviously reluctant to admit his stalking of Mallory to someone new.

"Sir, if it will make you feel more comfortable, I've been helping Detective Milligan with his investigation of this case."

"I suppose you know then that I was keeping pretty close tabs on Mallory. I knew most of the places she went and what she was doing. She met with Pastor Love on a regular basis."

"Did you know that she was being counseled by him?" It wasn't necessary to tell him, that according to Love, the counseling had begun because Mallory's husband hadn't taken Beltran's stalking seriously.

"Oh, it may have started that way, but it wasn't long before it turned into something else."

"Do you have proof of that?"

"I don't know what you call proof, but I could tell by the way they looked at each other. Many times, Pastor Love walked her to her car with his arm around her. He'd almost always give her a big hug before she got into her car."

"Did you ever see him kiss her?"

"Well, no. But he wouldn't be that obvious out in the parking lot of his church."

If he was worried about being seen, he wouldn't have hugged her in public either. Ministers were a huggy breed, at least she knew Reverend Cookmeyer hugged many of his flock, male and female.

"Is there anything else?" Stacey asked.

"No, but you be sure and tell Detective Milligan."

"I certainly will, and thank you. If you think of anything else, don't hesitate to call." Stacey hung up the phone. Beltran's information wasn't anything they didn't already know. She suspected the call was prompted by jealousy more than anything else, but she decided it wouldn't hurt to visit Pastor Love again.

* * *

Frank and Doug sat opposite Reverend Cookmeyer in his large office. Despite Frank's blunt and almost rude questions, Cookmeyer answered each one politely. Doug thought his partner was carrying the "good cop - bad cop" ploy to excess, as he asked the questions he'd already asked several times before.

"So tell me, Reverend, what kind of shape are your finances in? Been living beyond your means? Made any bad investments lately?" Frank scooted his chair forward so he was up against the desk.

"Hey, Frank, give him a chance to answer one question before you ask the next," Doug said.

"Okay, so what shape are your finances in?"

"Not as good as they could be." A slight crease marred Cookmeyer's smoothly tanned forehead. "Obviously Katherine's been talking to you. Yes, I have made some investments that didn't pay off. But no, I haven't been living beyond my means."

"Now that your wife's dead you'll be sitting pretty, isn't that right?"

"I have no idea what you mean, Detective."

"Oh, come on, Reverend. After all, you are the sole heir to your wife's estate. Isn't that right? We know all about Mrs. Cookmeyer's sizeable inheritance from her parents."

Reverend Cookmeyer actually smiled at Frank, surprising Doug. "I'm in mourning for my wife. I haven't even thought about her financial affairs. You can talk to our lawyer if you want the details of what I'll be inheriting." He scribbled on a piece of paper and slid it across the desk in Frank's direction. "Here's his name and phone number. I'm sure you can learn all you need to know from him. Now, is there anything else I can help you with?"

Frank folded the paper neatly and put it in the pocket of his shirt where he carried his gum. "Yes, actually there is. I understand you made a practice of leaving the door of your office open when you were counseling females. Is that right?"

"Since you seem to know so much about me and what I've done, I can tell Mrs. Danfelt has been very forthright with you. Yes, that's correct. Leaving the door ajar with my secretary outside at her desk is a form of insurance against false accusations."

Frank leaned as far as he could across the desk. "So why did you close the door when Sally Jo Roberts came to visit?"

"Is that what this is all about, my friendship with Sally Jo?" Cookmeyer was no longer smiling.

"Isn't that why you killed your wife, Reverend? You were in love with Sally Jo, and your wife was pregnant and wouldn't give you a divorce?"

Cookmeyer shook his head slowly. "No, Detective Marshall, none of what you said is true."

"Why don't you tell us what is," Doug urged.

"My relationship with Sally Jo is strictly as a minister and friend. I helped her through a particularly difficult part of her life, and I'm happy to say her way is much smoother now. I had no desire to marry her then, nor do I now."

Frank started to say something, but Doug jumped in first. "Reverend Cookmeyer, Miss Roberts told one of our officers that she's in love with you. Has she ever told you that?"

"I am well aware of what she thinks her feelings are. However, I've told her it's only because of the help I've given her. She's mistaking gratitude for love. However, it's quite normal for her to feel that way. It's similar to women who fall in love with the obstetricians who deliver their babies. Nevertheless, I can assure you, though I care for Sally Jo as a Christian sister and her minister, I do not return her romantic feelings, nor have I given her any cause to think that I do."

Frank leaned back in his chair and sneered.

"Since you were aware of Ms. Roberts' feelings

toward you, why did you shut the door when she visited you?" Doug asked. "Seems like you were asking for trouble."

"I did it because Katherine was becoming far too interested in Sally Jo. She poured out her heart to me. I didn't want anything she said to become gossip among the church members."

"You made a mistake," Doug said. "You may have protected her, but you exposed yourself. Whether you're aware of it or not, your church members are already linking you and Sally Jo romantically."

"Oh, I'm well aware of that. They'll soon quit talking when they finally realize that there isn't anything going on between us. I want you to understand I loved my wife. We got along fine. This is a demanding job. I imagine it's similar to yours. I'm called out during social engagements and the middle of the night for emergencies. Mallory may not have liked it, but she accepted it as part of what I do. She kept herself busy with her own interests."

Again Frank leaned forward. "What kind of interests were those, sir?"

Reverend Cookmeyer folded his hands on his desk and stared at them. "Well...ah...I must admit I don't actually know."

"Oh, I bet you do. You found out that she was having an affair, didn't you? And that's why you murdered her."

Chapter 16

Reverend Cookmeyer stood. "I did not murder my wife." It was obvious he was out of patience. "Unless there is something else, I have a lot of work to do. You ought to quit wasting my time and yours and start looking for the person who is responsible for my wife's death."

Frank raised himself from his chair, put both hands on the desk and leaned forward. "If you didn't do it because of the money or Sally Jo, was it because Mallory was pregnant and you knew it wasn't yours?"

Cookmeyer's usually placid expression turned formidable. "I think I've put up with enough of these false accusations, Detective. Unless you are planning to arrest me, please leave."

"Okay, for now." Frank squinted at the minister for a long minute before heading out the door.

"Thank you, Reverend," Doug said before

following him.

Mrs. Danfelt sat at her desk, a smug look on her face, leaving Doug with the impression that she'd had her ear to the door during their entire visit.

"We'll be back," Frank tossed in the secretary's direction.

She glowered at him. "No doubt."

Once outside, Doug said, "Don't you think you were a bit rough?"

Frank put a fresh stick of gum in his mouth. "Naw. He's tough. He can take it. Besides, he's still the best suspect except for that nasty old witch he has for a secretary. I wouldn't put anything past her. I wonder if he's lying about never having a fertility test?"

* * *

The dark brick edifice that housed All Saint's Calvary Church loomed out of the swirling fog. It seemed almost menacing. No wonder so many people had switched to Rocky Bluff Community with its modern architecture and safer location. Stacey had checked out a police unit and she parked it in the asphalt lot behind the two-story, square structure. Barred windows were at ground level as well as an opening to cement stairs that obviously led to a basement.

Another short flight of stairs with a banister went to a door with a sign that said, OFFICE. Giving a brief glance to the dark hole below, Stacey took the upward steps two at a time. The door was unlocked and Stacey stepped inside. A musty odor, not quite masked by the smell of pine-scented cleaner, greeted her. A dimly lit, narrow corridor led to several doors, all closed. The walls were paneled halfway with dark wood, the rest painted a sea foam green and decorated with fading posters with curled edges. Unfortunately, there were no windows and no lights except for the exit sign.

Stacey listened but heard nothing except her own footfalls as she started down the passageway. A crack of light under one of the doors drew her nearer. She was rewarded with another sign signifying she'd reached her goal.

She knocked. Before the door opened, she heard footsteps and papers being shuffled.

Pastor Love blinked in her direction before he peered past as though expecting someone else. "Officer Wilbur, isn't it?" His eyes flickered over her, and she knew he wondered why she wasn't in uniform.

It wasn't necessary to explain her promotion to him. "I thought Detectives Milligan and Marshall might be here."

"I haven't seen them, nor am I expecting them." The minister had regained his composure. "Is there something I can help you with?"

"If you don't mind, I'd like to talk to you a bit more about your counseling sessions with Mallory Cookmeyer." Stacey peered around him.

He smiled. "Would you like to come in? I don't have a full time secretary anymore. My wife does most of the secretarial chores these days." He stepped aside so she could enter.

Though free of dust, the area had an antiquated atmosphere. The one window was high and didn't let in much light. The desk was gray metal. It held nothing but an old computer, printer, and several large books—a Webster's dictionary, a Bible dictionary, a concordance, a Bible and a few others. There were two wooden file cabinets, a bookcase, and a desk chair. A worn rug covered the hardwood floor.

Pastor Love pointed the way into an inner office. It was larger with the same dark wood half way up the walls, but the remainder was papered in light yellow with a small green and brown abstract design. Framed diplomas and certificates were artfully arranged on the wall. A computer and printer sat on one end of the L-shaped desk. Papers and books were piled and scattered over the surface, along with an open laptop.

"Please, take a seat." He settled himself in a massive leather swivel chair while Stacey perched on the edge of a matching leather couch adorned with plump green and yellow pillows.

"Nice," Stacey said.

"Thanks to my wife." He folded his hands on top of his papers. "How can I help you?"

"I had an interesting phone call before I came here," Stacey began, watching Pastor Love carefully. As usual, what he had left of his dark hair was neatly cut and carefully combed. His tanned face was plump, clean-shaven and unblemished. His jacket was hanging on the back of his chair and he wore no tie. A light green, short-sleeved shirt exposed his tanned, muscular arms.

"I gather that phone call had something to do with me."

"Yes, it did. What do you know about a man named Louis Beltran?"

His eyes narrowed. "We're on shaky ground here. You know my counseling sessions with Mallory are privileged. Maybe you better tell me what you know about Mr. Beltran first."

"Okay, we can do it that way. We've learned from more than one source that Mr. Beltran was stalking Mallory Cookmeyer. So it stands to reason that he was the one she was having trouble with, and why she came to you for counseling in the first place. Right?"

"Yes, though I don't know that stalking was really the word for it, but he was certainly a pest and a persistent one at that. At first he was more annoying than threatening. But I still don't see what all this has to do..."

Stacey interrupted. "Louis Beltran called specifically to let us know that he thinks you and Mallory were having an affair."

"That's preposterous. Certainly you aren't going to give any credence to what that lunatic might say?" Though obviously annoyed, Pastor Love still had complete control of himself.

"We are investigating a murder, sir, so anything anyone might bring up needs to be checked. You understand that, don't you?"

"I understand the premise behind it, but I can't understand why you'd even bother with anything that idiot Beltran might make up."

"If you remember sir, your wife thought you might be having an affair with Mrs. Cookmeyer. When two people come up with the same notion, it's all the more intriguing, wouldn't you agree?"

"No, I wouldn't. The whole idea is asinine."

Before Stacey could say anything more, Hannah Love burst into the room. "I saw the police car and wondered if anything was wrong." With her curly red hair flying, and her brow furrowed, she gaped at Stacey. "What are you doing here? Why aren't you in uniform?"

Stacey received the immediate impression that Mrs. Love suspected her of trying to entice Pastor Love. She had to work at not laughing out loud. "My job doesn't require me to wear a uniform all the time, Mrs. Love. I came to ask your husband a few more questions."

"About what?" Hannah asked, still frowning.

"Officer Wilbur is investigating Mallory's murder, dear," Pastor Love said in a soothing voice. "I suppose we'll have to put up with these intrusions until they put her killer behind bars."

"I think it would be a really good idea if you and Mrs. Love went to the department and had your fingerprints taken. Would you be willing to do that?"

Mrs. Love stepped backwards and put her hands behind her back. "No. Why should we?"

Her husband stepped around his desk and put his arm around her. "Sure we will. Why not? Maybe it will help Officer Wilbur to realize we didn't have anything to do with Mallory's death. We'll do it right away. How's that?"

"Oh, I don't know…" Hannah murmured.

"Yes, you do. It'll only take a few minutes. Is that

all the questions you had for me?" Pastor Love asked.

There was one more she wanted to spring on him, but she didn't want to do it in front of his wife. She stood. "I'll let the dispatchers know you'll be coming in for the fingerprinting."

"We'll be there in a few minutes." The minister bestowed a smile of dismissal on Stacey, his arm still around his wife.

"I really don't want to have my fingerprints taken," Hannah said.

"Don't be silly, dear. It's absolutely painless. You'll see." He continued to reassure her as Stacey left the office.

She hoped Doug wouldn't be angry about her suggestion, but it seemed the logical thing to happen next. If neither Pastor nor Mrs. Love's prints matched any of the unknown prints they'd found in the car, it wouldn't completely clear them of suspicion, but it would help.

Doug still wasn't in his office by the time Stacey had notified the dispatcher that the Loves were coming in. She left a note in his office, explaining what she'd done. Though she would have liked to have waited for him, it was time she started interviewing prostitutes.

✳ ✳ ✳

"What's that all about?" Frank asked, as Doug frowned over the note he'd found on his desk.

"From Stacey. She's been to see Pastor Love again and his wife. Didn't find out a whole lot, but she sent them in to be fingerprinted. Mrs. Love wasn't exactly enthusiastic about the prospect."

"That Stacey is on the ball. I'll see if the Loves have been in yet."

At the bottom of her note, Stacey had written, "Will have an answer to your question soon, Love, S."

With his hand on the doorknob, Frank stared at him quizzically. "What else did she say?"

Doug quickly folded the note and stuck it in his pocket. "Nothing, just some personal stuff."

"Personal stuff, huh?" Frank grinned. "Things getting hot and heavy?"

"Not really." Though he hadn't meant to tell Frank yet, he blurted out, "I asked her to marry me."

"Hey, that's great. She said 'yes', didn't she?"

"Actually, she hasn't given me an answer yet."

Frank squeezed Doug's shoulder and winked. "Don't get all worried. I can see the sparks when you two are together. I'd put a week's paycheck on her saying 'yes'."

"Wish I felt as positive. There's her little boy to consider, you know."

"All the more reason for her to want to marry you. He likes you, doesn't he?"

"Sure, and I like him too. There's also her folks."

"For crying out loud, Doug, Stacey's a grown-up. Her parents aren't going to stand in her way. Besides, they like you too, don't they?"

"I think so."

"She's probably just playing hard-to-get. Women like to do that."

"No, that's something Stacey wouldn't do."

"Then you're worrying for nothing, man."

"I hope so. I really love her, Frank."

"I know you do."

"Think I'll see if I can find her somewhere. She said in her note she was looking for us when she decided to make her call on Pastor Love."

Frank grinned again. "Sure, buddy, you do that."

Chapter 17

Playing a hunch, Doug drove back to the bluffs. Cruising slowly past Rocky Bluff Community Church, he was surprised to see Reverend Cookmeyer's car was no longer in the parking lot. Stepping on the accelerator, Doug headed toward Cookmeyer's home.

"Well, well, what have we here?"

Cookmeyer's car was in the driveway. Parked next to the curb in front of the house was a red Mustang. Stacey had told him that Sally Jo Roberts drove one. Pulling in behind it, Doug radioed in the license number. In minutes, his suspicions were confirmed. Finding the choir director's car at Cookmeyer's belied both the minister's and her protestations that they were merely friends, not lovers.

Doug had to ring the bell twice before the door opened.

Cookmeyer glowered at him through the screen

door. "What is this, Detective? I've been extremely patient with you and your partner. You are coming dangerously close to police harassment."

"Aren't you overreacting? I'm curious about your company, is all. Isn't that Sally Jo Roberts' car?"

"What if it is? That's not any of your business, Detective Milligan."

"It's very much my business. Both you and Miss Roberts have been trying to convince us that nothing has been going on between you, and now I find you entertaining her in your home. What am I supposed to think about that?"

Reverend Cookmeyer's deep tan had turned an unhealthy shade of maroon. "I want you to leave," he growled.

Sally Jo, her eyes red-rimmed pushed past him. "I'm going too. I'm so sorry, Paul. I should have listened to you and stayed away. I don't want to cause you any more trouble. I only wanted you to know how badly I feel about all this."

"It's all right, truly it is. If Detective Milligan wants to make something out of a short, daytime visit, so be it. You and I and the Lord know there wasn't more to it." Cookmeyer reached out to her, but she rushed past both of them and ran across the lawn to her car. The sound of her sobbing coming back to them.

"Now you've upset her," Cookmeyer scolded.

But Doug concluded it was probably Cookmeyer's words that had provoked Sally Jo's tears.

* * *

"Glad you made it back so soon. Have some interesting news for you," Frank said as Doug entered his office. "Don't sit down. We have a call to make."

"On who?"

"Mrs. Hannah Love." Frank grinned.

Doug knew exactly what had happened. "Well, I'll be. Her fingerprints match some of those in Mallory Cookmeyer's car."

"You've got it. Our sweet little pastor's wife has got some explaining to do."

* * *

Hannah Love was as about as enthusiastic as Reverend Cookmeyer had been about the detectives' visit, though she was more hospitable.

"I can't imagine what you could possible want with me. I've answered so many questions already." She sighed but opened the door wider. "I suppose you can come in..." Her voice trailed off.

She walked into the middle of the crowded living room, and using both hands, shoved back her thick red hair. She sounded weary as she said, "What is it now?"

Frank moved quite close to her. "We matched your fingerprints to several that we found in Mallory Cookmeyer's car. What do you have to say about that, Mrs. Love?"

Her reaction came slowly. Her whole body began shaking, imperceptibly at first and then more pronounced. Her face turned bright pink beneath her freckles. At first, Doug thought she was extremely angry.

Hannah swayed. Her knees buckled. Frank reached out, grabbed her, and helped her to the couch, where she collapsed. Her breathing came in ragged gasps. Doug changed his opinion, realizing Hannah Love was frightened.

"Are you going to be all right?" Frank asked, his forehead furrowed. His "bad cop" demeanor vanished.

She sobbed loudly, hands covering her face.

With a puzzled expression, Frank turned toward Doug.

Doug sat beside her and touched her shoulder.

"Do you want me to get your husband?"

"No," she cried, lifting her tear-streaked face.

"Do you think you can answer our questions now?"

"I...I'll try." She fished a tissue from her skirt pocket and blotted her eyes and nose. "What do you want to know?"

"Why were your fingerprints in Mallory Cookmeyer's wrecked car?" Doug asked.

"Oh, my dear God," she said.

Doug knew her plea was truly directed toward heaven.

"If Joshua finds out he'll be so mad at me."

"What is it you don't want your husband to find out, Mrs. Love?" Doug prompted.

She acted like she hadn't heard him. "He won't understand, I know. He never understood how it made me feel when he spent so much time with that beautiful woman. It didn't matter how much he reassured me, I couldn't help remembering that he betrayed me once before."

Was she going to make a confession right here and now? Doug hadn't expected this, and he could tell by Frank's startled expression, he didn't either.

Hannah continued. "It seemed like he spent more time with her than he did with me. She even called him here at the house. He always took the phone into the other room so I couldn't hear. He said it was because of confidentiality, but I knew better. He didn't want me to hear when he used words of love to her."

"Did you ever hear him do that?" Frank asked.

Though she didn't look at the detective, she answered. "No, but I didn't have to. I knew what was going on between them. I could see the guilt in his eyes...smell her perfume on him..."

She began crying again.

Doug cleared his throat. "Mrs. Love...." He shrugged his shoulders at Frank. "Please, you have to tell us how your fingerprints got into Mallory

Cookmeyer's car."

Chapter 18

Hannah Love sniffed and raised her moist face, her eyes wet with tears. "Mallory was supposed to have a counseling session with my husband and I intercepted her when she arrived in the parking lot."

"How did you know about the session?" Doug asked, quietly.

"I listened in when she called him. She sounded desperate. Said she had to talk to him. Ha. That's what she always said."

"Why don't you tell us exactly what happened, Hannah?"

If she did confess to them, Doug felt they could get her to say it all over again at the station. But if they stopped her now, she might clam up after she had her emotions under control.

"I was waiting when she pulled in. Before she got out, I jumped into the passenger side of her car. She didn't act all that surprised. "'Why don't you go someplace where we can have a private conversation', I said. And she smiled at me. 'Sure', she said. She drove around a bit, and finally parked near the old pier. 'How's this?' she asked.

"I didn't care. I just wanted to be some place private. We sat there for a long time, watching the waves crash on the shore. The sand swirled in the wind. The longer I sat there, the harder it was for me to know what to say. Finally, she was the one who began. 'I think I know what this is all about.'

"'Oh, you do, do you. Why don't you tell me then?' I said. She did and I couldn't believe what she said. She admitted that she and Joshua were having an affair. She came right out and told me that they loved each other. She said they planned to marry, and asked if he'd told me yet."

"And he hadn't," Frank put in.

"No, of course not. He always insisted nothing was going on between them."

"What did you do then?"

Her far-off gaze and agonized expression told Doug she was reliving the painful memory.

"I was stunned. I didn't know what to do or say. You have no idea how shocked I was. Though I suspected Joshua, deep down I hoped he'd been telling me the truth. Now that it was all out in the open, I wasn't sure how I felt. But Mallory kept right on. With every word it was like she was twisting a knife in my heart."

When it seemed like she had submerged herself in the painful memory, Doug nudged her verbally with, "Can you remember what she told you?"

"Every hurtful word."

"Tell us," he said.

She shook her head even though she began again. "I've tried to get it out of my mind. Maybe none of it was true, maybe it was just what she wanted to believe. If only I had the nerve to confront Joshua, but I can't bring myself to do that."

Joshua didn't know about this meeting between his wife and his lover? "What exactly did she say, Hannah?"

"It hurts. You have no idea how much." She turned her tear-stained face toward Doug. "I'll probably never forget how I felt when she told me that my husband wanted to divorce me and marry her. Mallory was surprised he hadn't told me yet. That wasn't the worst of it."

Doug could see that Frank was getting impatient, but they needed to be gentle with Hannah so she would tell them everything. "Of course we can't know how horrible this was for you. What happened then?"

"I was stunned. I couldn't think of anything to say. What came next was the worst of all." She started to cry again. "She said she was pregnant with Joshua's baby. I begged and begged him to have another child with me, and he wouldn't do it. If he was having a baby with Mallory, I wanted to die right there and then. Except for the death of Kimberly Ann, that was the worst thing that ever happened to me in my whole life. I got out of the car and began running down the beach. I didn't pay attention to where I was going. After a while, I found myself downtown, not too far from home. But I couldn't go there, I was too upset. I needed time to think. That's when I went to the movie. I didn't even see what was going on, all I could do was think about what Mallory told me."

"Ha." Frank exploded. "You expect us to believe that? You find out this woman had an affair with your husband and is pregnant with his baby, and you just ran away? I don't think so."

She whirled around. "Well, it's true. I told you exactly what happened."

"I think it went down like this," Frank said. "I bet you've been listening in on your husband's phone calls with Mallory right along, and you knew about their affair. You finally had enough and you arranged this little meeting with her. You went up in the hills and shot her in the head. Gave the car a shove to make it look like an accident, then made your way back home. Isn't that the way it was, Mrs. Love?"

Hannah frowned. "No. That's crazy. I didn't kill her." She turned toward Doug. "You don't think that, do you, Detective Milligan?"

"I'm not sure what to think. If you did kill her, it would be much better for you to admit it now."

Hannah jumped to her feet. "I did not kill Mallory Cookmeyer. God forgive me, I'm certainly not sorry that she's gone, but I didn't kill her. I couldn't kill anyone."

Frank stood and stared menacingly at her. "Maybe you should come down to the station with us."

"What for? I've told you exactly what happened." She began backing away from him. "I don't have to go anywhere."

"No, you don't," Doug said, knowing that her fingerprints were the only evidence they had against her. Certainly not enough for an arrest. He had expected her to confess. When she didn't, he felt he needed to look elsewhere. "Tell me, Hannah, when you came home, was your husband here?"

"Yes, he was."

"Do you know what time it was?"

"Not really. I sat in the movie thinking, but I didn't stay until it was over. I was too upset to notice the time."

"Did you confront Joshua with what you learned from Mallory?"

"No. He was waiting for me in the living room. Asked where I'd been, said he was worried about me. He acted so happy to see me, took me in his arms and kissed me. I felt that Mallory lied to me about everything. Oh, she wanted my husband all right, but she wasn't having any luck with him, so she was going to work on me. She lied about the affair and she lied about the pregnancy."

Doug made sure Hannah was looking directly at

him when he said, "Mallory was three months pregnant when she died."

"Oh, my God," Hannah gasped. She blinked several times, before saying, "That doesn't mean it was Joshua's, does it?'

"No, we don't know who the father was...yet."

Quickly regaining her composure, Hannah said, "It's not Joshua's. I know it. He was so afraid if we had another child it would have Down Syndrome like our little girl. He would never take that chance."

"Thank you, Mrs. Love," Doug began, "we've bothered you enough. If you think of anything else, be sure to call." He took hold of Frank's upper arm and began steering him toward the door.

Heading for their car, Frank said, "She did it. I know she did. She had the means and the motive. It had to be her. All we needed to do was lean on her more. She would've cracked. I know she would."

"Maybe. But we really don't have enough evidence. We should run this by Chief McKenzie first, because you know what? I think she's telling the truth."

"If she is, then it's her husband we ought to be talking to," Frank said. He stared toward the massive brick church. The parking lot was empty and the church was dark.

"My feeling exactly, but it doesn't look like anyone is there."

Frank glanced at his watch. "It's getting late. I suppose it can wait until tomorrow. I doubt if Mrs. Love is going to confront her husband about his affair with the dead woman."

* * *

Already late for the boys' football game, Ryan Strickland was waylaid outside of the department by one of the *Banner's* reporters, a skinny guy named Harold something or other. "Hey, Strickland. What's the latest on the Cookmeyer murder case? Arrested anyone yet?"

"No, 'fraid not, Harold," Ryan said, not breaking his stride as he hurried toward his car.

"So who's the favored suspect? The husband?"

"Don't know. Sorry."

"Hey, and what about this Truesdale suicide? Is it true there wasn't a note. Isn't that kind of suspicious?"

"Unusual, yes. Suspicious, no." Ryan didn't want to make Harold angry. He'd always managed to get along with the press, and he knew that keeping them happy was far better for the department. "What we put in the press release about Evan Truesdale's suicide is really all we know at this time. This is extremely difficult for his family. We really don't know anymore."

Harold shook his head. "You're keeping something back, I can feel it."

"Sorry, we'd like to know too. Maybe Mr. Truesdale found out he had some kind of incurable cancer or something."

"Anyone check with his doctor about that?"

"No, but it's just an idea." Pretty good one at that. Could have happened that way. And to appease the reporter even more, Ryan said, "I think we're getting close on the Cookmeyer case. I promise I'll let you know as soon as I hear something."

He unlocked the door of his Lexus. "I've got to go now. I'm late for my son's football game. Wife's going to be pretty unhappy with me." Barbara wouldn't be, she'd be glad he showed up at all, but anything to help his escape from the newsman.

＊ ＊ ＊

Stacey spent most of the afternoon and on into the early evening talking to prostitutes and street people, showing cropped copies of the pictures Evan Truesdale had kept in his album. No one she talked to recognized the child. Knowing that the photographs were a couple of years old, they probably were taken in the Los Angeles area where the Truesdales lived before coming to Rocky Bluff. Tomorrow she would call down there, to try to interest someone in following up.

Hoping to catch Doug, she returned to the station, but was disappointed to find out he'd already checked out for the day. Everyone was all a buzz with the news that Hannah Love's fingerprints matched some of those found in Mallory Cookmeyer's car.

Though she knew she ought to go home, she still wanted to talk to Doug and find out if he'd gotten anywhere on the Cookmeyer case. She'd been thinking a lot about Doug's proposal. Being married to him would be wonderful. Maybe she'd stop by his house and give him her answer.

* * *

Gordon Butler responded to a burglary call that turned out to be nothing more than a house cat that upset a lamp of an extremely nervous old lady. After that, all was quiet. He drove up and down the streets without spotting anyone even bending a traffic law.

He continued covering the area he was assigned to, mostly middle and upper class neighborhoods where nothing much happened. How he longed for some action. Maybe he ought to transfer to a big city where they had more crime. Yeah, that's what he would do. Might help the social part of his life too.

The only woman he'd been interested in since his wife left him was Stacey. It was obvious Stacey and Doug were in love. He should have seen it coming. Oh, well, they made a nice couple.

Nearing the end of an alley, he spotted something strange. Braking, he switched on his spotlight and played it over what looked like a twisted body jammed between two trash cans. "Oh, boy."

Leaving the engine running, he dashed toward the victim whose legs were splayed in an unnatural position. "Hey, man, are you okay?"

He shined his flashlight in the direction where the head should be and realized what he was looking at was a life-size dummy. Jeans and shirt stuffed with rags, stuffed pillowcase for a head. "Kids' idea of a joke, I suppose."

Splashing the beam all around, Gordon reassured himself no one was in the alley ready to explode with laughter. To prevent anyone else mistaking the dummy for a human, he carried it back to his unit and placed it in an upright position in the back seat.

"Well, buddy, you just sit tight." He chuckled to himself, at least his "prisoner" would give his fellow officers something to laugh about.

He whipped around the corner, and the dummy fell over. He pulled next to the curb, climbed out, opened up the back seat and yanked the dummy upright, and laughing, gave it a punch. "Behave yourself or I'll knock the stuffing out of you."

He heard a noise and saw a diminutive, white-haired figure standing on a front porch. It was an old woman.

"Howdy, ma'am," he greeted. "Nice evening, isn't it?"

The woman fled inside her house.

Chapter 19

Stacey couldn't help smiling as she turned down Doug's street. She hoped he would be as pleased with her decision as she was. Actually, she was surprised that she'd made it so quickly, but she couldn't imagine anyone she'd rather marry. Though her parents would be surprised too, they would be happy for her.

When she pulled up in front of the restored Victorian, she was disappointed to see that the windows were dark and Doug's MG wasn't in the driveway. Where could he be? She realized she didn't know a whole lot about his private life. He loved his home and put a lot of effort into its upkeep. He spent a lot of time working on his car and was a great cook. Other than his love for law enforcement, she didn't know how else he occupied himself. Perhaps she didn't know him well enough to marry him. It didn't matter now; he wasn't home and she had more time to think about her answer.

Turning her VW around in the middle of the block, she thought about where he might be. She knew he would have questioned Hannah Love today about her fingerprints in Mallory Cookmeyer's Toyota.

All the suspects' fingerprints had turned up in the car: Reverend Paul Cookmeyer, Katherine Danfelt, Sally Jo Roberts, and Hannah Love. Everyone's fingerprints were there except for Pastor Love's.

She thought about that for a moment and then she had an idea. She needed to find Doug and talk to him. Maybe he was still at the Loves' house. Driving quickly back down town toward All Saint's Community church and the parsonage, Stacey felt happy, happier than she'd been in a long while. She could hardly wait to see Doug, and when the time was right, she'd give him her decision.

No car was parked in front of the parsonage. What was she thinking? He wouldn't be driving his MG if he was working. She pulled into the parking lot. Only one car was there, a late model Jeep that Stacey knew belonged to Joshua Love. That meant he was still in the church. Though the light was on over the rear door and one of the windows was lit, the building wasn't particularly inviting.

Should she go inside and talk to Pastor Love? Maybe she could catch him off guard and find out something incriminating. She didn't have to let on what she instinctively knew to be true.

Before she could make up her mind, a heavy hand grasped her shoulder. "What are you doing?" It was Pastor Love.

Her heartbeat quickened. "Goodness, you startled me."

Love glowered at her. "I'm getting awfully tired of this. We've been more than patient with all of you, but this harassment has got to stop."

Smiling, her voice a pretense of sweetness, she said, "You're overreacting, sir. I was just looking for someone."

"Really. In my church's parking lot." He still gripped her shoulder.

"That's right. But since we're both here, perhaps there's something more you'd like to tell me."

His fingers dug into her flesh, but she forced herself not to react.

He was quiet for a moment, then his voice and demeanor changed. "Perhaps if we sit down and talk sensibly, you'll finally see that you're going after the wrong person here. My wife would never harm anyone. I can't imagine why you people are even considering her as a suspect."

"Did you know that your wife's fingerprints matched some that were found on Mallory Cookmeyer's car?"

His round face registered genuine surprise. "No. That can't be. There has to be a mistake."

"No, sir. I assure you there isn't."

He glanced toward his home. "Let's go inside the sanctuary." He put his hand on the small of her back and guided her, a bit forcefully, toward the stairs.

Once inside, the poor lighting of the hallway did nothing to reassure Stacey. "I can't stay very long, Pastor Love. I'm overdue at home."

"This shouldn't take more than a few minutes." He pushed her toward the nearest door. "Go on in there."

The hall opened into a dark room that smelled of furniture polish, dying flowers, and mold. Pastor Love reached for the wall and turned on lights over a raised stage. Only the choir loft, the altar, and the first three rows of dark wooden pews were illuminated. "Sit down." His voice echoed as he motioned to the first maroon padded bench.

"I've never been here before," Stacey said, glancing around. Even though it was dark, she sensed the room was cavernous. The seats and backs of the choir benches showed signs of wear as did the cream colored curtains draping the back wall.

With his arms crossed over his massive chest,

Pastor Love stood in front of her. "I suppose you attend Cookmeyer's church on the bluff."

"Yes, sir, I do," Stacey said.

"I'm not surprised. Flashy building in the snob part of town."

As long as she was there, she might as well prod him a bit. "I bet you really have it in for Reverend Cookmeyer, the way he stole all your church members."

"You don't know the half of it, lady."

"Why don't you tell me?" Stacey said.

"We had it really good here for a while." He smiled though Stacey thought she spotted tears glistening in his eyes. "Except for the Catholics and the Jews, this was the church that people who were somebody in the community attended. Some Sundays there was standing room only. City leaders came to me for advice about political matters. Whoever I endorsed got elected to office."

He whirled back around to face her. "But it all changed when Cookmeyer arrived. My church members began slipping away, at first only one family at time. Then they bailed out in droves. I couldn't believe they would be so disloyal. I visited each one, tried to find out what had happened. But they didn't have any answers. Oh, one woman told me that 'I didn't feed her spirit like Reverend Cookmeyer', whatever that was supposed to mean."

Eyes blazing, Love lowered his voice. "No, Cookmeyer conspired against me. He lured away my flock with promises he couldn't possibly keep."

Stacey tried to imagine what kind of promises and guessed there probably hadn't been any. She plunged ahead with a change in subject. "You know, Pastor Love, I've been thinking a lot about Mallory Cookmeyer's murder and the fingerprints they found in the car. What I'm curious about is not whose fingerprints were in the car, but those that weren't."

He stared at her with his eyebrows nearly touching. "I have no idea what you mean."

"Well, sir, think about it for a minute. It seems terribly strange to me that not one single print of yours turned up in Mallory's Toyota."

His answer came quickly. "But why would they? I never went anywhere with Mallory."

"I'm not so sure that's true, but even if it is, surely you opened her car door for her a time or two. I can't believe you never touched the inside of her car."

His frown deepened.

Stacey clicked her tongue against the roof of her mouth. "What I think happened is that the person who shot Mallory probably wore gloves or very carefully wiped away his fingerprints. Someone who was a former police officer would know not to leave fingerprints behind."

"My goodness, Officer Wilbur, you certainly have a wild imagination. What kind of a motive could I possibly have had to do such a horrible thing?" He moved closer to the large mahogany pulpit and leaned against it.

"Perhaps it was your way of getting back at Reverend Cookmeyer."

Pastor Love laughed. "Rather drastic retribution, don't you think? I'm certainly not thrilled by the way he stole so many of my congregation, but no one in his right mind would believe that I would murder his wife for revenge. That doesn't make sense."

"H'mmm, maybe not, but it'll do until you tell me the real reason."

"You've made up your mind that I killed Mallory and nothing is going to convince you differently." Beads of perspiration dotted his upper lip. "You really aren't as smart as you think you are."

"You're right. If I were really smart I'd be able to figure out why you did it." Stacey glanced around. This was headed toward resolution much faster than she'd expected. She should have let someone know where she was going. He surprised her with his next remark.

"I do love my wife. Hannah has stood by me

through everything. She was right there when I had to leave the police department. She encouraged me when members of my congregation slipped away." He stared out into the blackness of the sanctuary.

Now was the time to get the hell out of there, but curiosity got the better of her. Stacey wanted to hear what else he had to say.

Pastor Love turned toward her. "Did you know we had a daughter?"

Stacey nodded.

"She had Down Syndrome. Sweet little girl. Hannah was crazy about her. When she died I wondered if I might lose my wife too. I couldn't put her through anything else."

"What else was there?"

He continued as though he hadn't heard her. "The scandal would have finished me as a minister. I can never go back to law enforcement. I couldn't let her ruin that for me."

"Who are you talking about?" Stacey asked.

He blinked as though he'd forgotten about her. "Why Mallory, of course. She was pregnant with my child. She wanted to divorce Paul and marry me. I told her to get rid of the baby, I had no desire to marry her."

As much as Stacey knew she ought to get out, she had to hear it all. "What did she say?"

"She planned to keep the baby, pass it off as Paul's. But that wouldn't work because she'd told me that she and Paul weren't having sex. He would know it wasn't his child. And there was always the chance it might be born with Down Syndrome."

Without thinking, Stacey asked, "Is that why you murdered Mallory?"

He stuck his hand into a narrow shelf in the pulpit and yanked out a revolver. "Unfortunately you've arrived at a conclusion that means you must die. I probably should have gotten rid of the gun earlier, but now I'm glad I didn't. I'll take care of you and then dump you and the gun into the ocean."

The situation had gotten far worse that she had anticipated. "You'll never get away with that."

"Oh, but I will. No one but you suspects me. Why would they connect me to your unfortunate demise?"

Her mind darted about, seeking ways to save herself. He was far too strong for her to take his gun away, and if she ran, he'd shoot her. He was going to kill her either way.

* * *

Doug went shopping on the way home, picking up the week's supply of groceries. He chose a couple of great looking salmon steaks, thinking of inviting Stacey over for dinner. With that in mind, he found some brown rice and salad fixings to serve with the fish, smiling as he planned the meal.

After his purchases were loaded in the passenger seat and boot of his M.G., he drove to Stacey's. He could hardly wait for her answer to his proposal. She'd asked for time to think about it, but maybe she'd decided. It wouldn't hurt to turn up on her doorstep. He'd use the dinner invitation as his excuse for being there.

Grinning with hopeful anticipation, he put the M.G. in gear and sped off in the direction of Stacey's home.

* * *

Gordon was about to call in to request time for his dinner break, when his radio came to life. The dispatcher ordered him to report to the Watch Commander immediately.

"Wonder what's happening?" Maybe there was some excitement he could get in on. Driving exactly the speed limit, he headed toward the station.

Abel Navarro and Lt. Stafford waited for him in the briefing room. Neither one smiled as he greeted them with, "What's up?"

Stafford had one eyebrow raised, and his mouth was a straight line. A single crease marred Abel's forehead.

"We've had a complaint about you, Butler," the lieutenant said.

Gordon was shocked. "Me? Why that's impossible? I haven't given out a single ticket so far this shift."

"This is a lot more serious than a ticket," Abel said.

This was crazy. "I have no idea what you're talking about."

"Someone has reported you for police brutality," Stafford explained.

"To make matters worse, you haven't logged in any calls." Abel stared at him.

"Police brutality. That's insane. I haven't even been in contact with..." Then it became clear: the dummy in the back seat, the little old lady on the porch. Gordon guffawed.

Abel grabbed Gordon's upper arm and shook it. "Hey, Gordon, this isn't a laughing matter. You know how people feel about police brutality. You could lose your job over this, man."

It took a minute or two before Gordon could control his outburst. He chortled throughout his explanation. "I found a dummy. That's what your caller saw. It kept falling over and I did punch it, but it's just a dummy."

Stafford's frown deepened. "A dummy, you say? Can you prove it?"

"Sure, I can. I've got it in the back seat of my unit. Come out and take a look."

* * *

Doug had stopped by Stacey's, but her VW bug wasn't in the driveway. Disappointed, he went home. After putting the groceries away, he decided to call her.

Stacey's mother answered. "Sorry, Doug, but Stacey hasn't come home from work yet."

Surprised, he asked, "Did she call, tell you when to expect her?"

"No, but she has this new job now, you know. She told us that she would be working erratic hours. Is something wrong?"

"No. I'm trying to locate her, is all. When she comes home, will you tell her I called?"

"Of course, Doug."

He hung up, disturbed by what Clare had told him. Nobody had mentioned anything Stacey was working on. Surely she wasn't still trying to find out the identity of the little girl in the photographs. That was a rather futile exercise anyway, and she hadn't sounded as though she expected a resolution.

What else could she be doing? Something to do with the Cookmeyer case, maybe. She was fascinated by it. The last thing he'd told her was about finding Hannah Love's fingerprints in the car. Surely she wouldn't go there on her own.

But she'd done it before.

If Pastor Love was the guilty party like Frank suggested, and Stacey had come to the same conclusion, maybe she was investigating the preacher on her own. If he did kill a preacher's wife, he wouldn't have any problem harming Stacey.

Doug grabbed his car keys, instinctively his hand went to his gun in the shoulder holster as he dashed through the house, slamming the front door behind him.

Dear God, he hoped he was wrong.

Chapter 20

The door banged open and Hannah stepped into the light, long red tendrils flying wildly around her head. "It's true then? You were having a baby with Mallory? Oh, Joshua, how could you?"

In that instant his attention was drawn to his wife, Stacey hurled herself at his gun hand. She connected with the full force of her weight and knocked the revolver from his grasp. He dived toward it. Hannah screamed. Stacey dashed across the stage toward a door at the opposite end.

She flung it open and darted through into an even darker area.

"You might as well stop, I'm going to get you," Pastor Love shouted, his heavy footfalls vibrating behind her.

"Joshua, please. Don't make it any worse than it already is," Hannah cried.

"I did this all for you," Joshua said. "Don't you understand?"

The preacher had the advantage. He knew his way around the building. Stacey didn't, and she couldn't see where she was going. Running along with both hands outstretched, she felt another door. Pulling it open, she slipped inside and let it fall closed. Reaching out, she realized she was at the top of a staircase leading downward. Damn.

There was no turning back. Feeling along a wooden banister, she scurried down the steps. When she reached the bottom, she paused for a moment, hoping her eyes would soon adjust to the darkness. The only light came from far away, one of the few high windows she'd spotted from the outside.

She bumped into something, felt it and realized it was a long table. Hurrying beside it, she struck a metal chair that pushed against the table with a resounding clang.

The door at the top of the staircase opened, and Joshua Love's bulky body was silhouetted in the dim light. "I know you're down there," he said. "You can't get away from me."

Maybe not, but she was going to give it a valiant try. Guessing that the room contained more tables and chairs, Stacey moved slowly, placing her feet carefully so as not to bang against any more of them. Love might know what was down here, but he couldn't see any better than she could. Of course, there was always the possibility that he might turn on the light, but she hoped he wouldn't, not wanting to attract attention to unusual activity going on in the church.

Stacey's heart pounded so hard she was afraid Love would hear. Along with that frightening sound, she heard his heavy footsteps on the stairs.

Finally, away from the tables, Stacey headed toward the light hoping to find the way out.

Pastor Love wasn't worrying about making noise as he banged against the chairs, hurling some out of his way with a resounding clatter. "I'm going to get you."

Because he was so noisy he wouldn't hear her, she darted across an open space. She found herself at a stairwell leading upward. The dim light showed a door at the top. Gasping as she darted up the steps, she threw herself at the bar crossing the door. It didn't budge. She tried again, no luck.

A shot rang out. She ducked. The bullet clanged against the metal door.

"You can't escape that way. There's a padlock on the outside." His maniacal laugh echoed in the large basement room.

"Oh, my God, Joshua." Hannah screamed from somewhere behind him. "Stop this madness now."

Stacey leapt over the banister, landing hard. She darted off into the deeper shadows. The man was crazed. She couldn't hide from him forever. Once he got tired of chasing after her in the dark, no doubt he'd turn on the lights. Then it would be all over.

The only way to win was to go on the offensive. Feeling her way along the wall, she came to a door that stood slightly ajar. Crouching down, she scooted inside. The strong odor of pine-scented cleaner assaulted her. Her fingers brushed against a broom handle. Beside the broom was a large, metal mop bucket. Perfect.

Picking it up, she stood. Remaining behind the protection of the door, Stacey waited.

Pastor Love called out to her. "There's no way out of here. If you're hiding in the furnace room, I'll kill you, and throw your body in the old furnace. We don't use it anymore and no one will ever think of looking for you there." He moved closer.

She gripped the bucket firmly in her hands.

For a moment, she couldn't hear anything except Hannah sobbing in the distance. But she knew Love was listening for her like she listened for him. She tried not to breathe.

A stealthy footfall sounded far too close to Stacey's hiding place. Keep coming, you bastard.

Another step, and she could smell mint aftershave and deodorant not quite covering the acrid scent of sweat.

She leapt around the door, bucket raised upside down. Pastor Love stood right in front of her.

"There you..."

But the rest of his words were muffled as she leaped up and smashed the heavy bucket down hard over his head. She shoved his gun hand away as it fired.

He dropped to his knees.

Stacey stomped on the preacher's hand.

He released his grip.

She scooped up the gun. "It's all over, Pastor."

The overhead lights blazed on. Doug's voice rang out, "Stacey. What the heck's going on?"

"I've got Mallory Cookmeyer's murderer," Stacey cried.

"I'll get you for this," Pastor' Love's muffled words came from inside the bucket.

"Relax, Pastor Love. You're under arrest for the murder of Mallory Cookmeyer."

Doug pushed his way past the hysterically crying Hannah Love. He ran to Stacey's side and yanked the bucket off Pastor Love's head. It clattered to the floor.

As the preacher started to rise, Doug pushed him back to his knees. "Stay right where you are." Quickly, he pulled Pastor Love's arms around to his back and handcuffed him.

"Joshua Love admitted killing Mallory Cookmeyer. And he was doing his best to kill me."

"Don't believe her," Pastor Love said, "She's making everything up. She came to the church and accosted my wife."

"Oh, Joshua," Hannah howled.

"Good work, Stacey," Doug said, pulling a printed card from his suit jacket." You have the right to be silent. Whatever you say can and will be held..." When Doug had finished reading Love his rights, he said, "Grab my cell phone, Stacey, and call for back-up."

"You've got it all wrong," Pastor Love pleaded. "It's this woman here who's caused all the trouble. You've got to listen to me. Ask my wife. She'll tell you, won't you, sweetheart?"

Hannah howled all the louder.

Doug ignored Love's ongoing protests and his wife's shrieks. Grinning at Stacey, he asked, "What made you realize he was the killer?"

"Of all the suspects, his fingerprints were the only ones not in Mallory's car..." Stacey began.

"Because he was a former policeman he had sense enough not to leave fingerprints behind," Doug added. "Unfortunately, I didn't think of that quick enough."

"I'd say the timing was perfect." Stacey grinned at him.

A siren sounded in the distance, growing louder and joined by another. Both stopped close by.

Love tried once more to wrench his way from Doug's grasp. "Hey. Settle down," Doug warned.

"But you've got to listen to me," Pastor Love pleaded. "It's all been a misunderstanding." He stared at his wife. "Tell them, sweetheart, you know I wouldn't kill anyone."

Hannah stood at the top of the stairs. "No, Joshua, I'm not lying for you again. When you were a police officer and were accused of raping that woman, I lied for you because you said you didn't do it. You've hurt me for the last time. I'm not lying about murder."

"Hannah, I love you." Love cried out. "How can you do this to me?"

"If you loved me, how could you have done this to me? You knew I wanted another baby. How could you kill a woman who was pregnant with your child? It's all too horrible. " Hannah glared at her husband before disappearing through the door.

Above them, doors banged, heavy steps reverberated overhead, followed by shouts.

"Hey, Milligan."

"Wilbur, where are you?"

"Down here." Doug hauled Love to his feet and pushed him in the direction of the stairs to the main floor. Before they reached the first step, Gordon Butler clattered down, gun drawn, with Abel Navarro and Lieutenant Stafford on his heels.

* * *

Once Joshua Love was booked and safely tucked away in a jail cell, Doug called Ryan Strickland. "We got Mallory Cookmeyer's murderer."

"Great. Who is it?"

"Pastor Joshua Love."

"Hey, that's a surprise."

"Chief McKenzie wants us to all meet with him in the morning. He'll give his go-ahead on a press release then."

"So what was Love's motive?"

"The baby Mallory Cookmeyer was carrying was his. She wanted to marry him, but that wasn't in his plan. He thought about just letting her go ahead and have it, but because of his counseling sessions with her, he knew she wasn't having sex with her husband. There was always the chance, no matter how slight, that he just might have fathered another child with Down Syndrome. He didn't think he could fool his wife about that."

"How'd he do it?"

"He isn't admitting anything, but the way Stacey has it figured out from what his wife said, Mrs. Love intercepted Mallory and went off with her first. When Mallory came back to the church for her counseling session, the Pastor jumped in the car with her. Had her drive to the foothills, shot her, and rigged the car so it would plow into the tree. He hiked about a mile before hitching a ride back to the church. With any luck, once all this gets out, whoever picked him up will come forward. Love was fortunate enough to make it back home before his wife did."

"Have you got enough real evidence?" Strickland asked.

"He confessed to Stacey. Of course he's calling her a liar, but we do have the gun, that ought to be evidence enough. I wouldn't be at all surprised if Hannah Love testifies against her husband."

"The media will have a field day with this one," Ryan said. "Maybe they'll forget all about the Truesdale suicide."

When he got off the phone, Doug turned to Stacey," Why don't we go back to my place for a cup of coffee?"

"I really ought to go home. My folks are probably worried," Stacey said, though she really did want to tell Doug about her decision.

"You can call them from my house," Doug said.

"Okay, I'll follow you over." She started to leave, but hesitated. "Oh, darn, my car is still parked in the church parking lot."

"Don't worry. You can ride with me. We can take care of your car in the morning."

* * *

Gordon could hardly wait to rehash Joshua Love's capture and arrest. The living room light was on, he hoped Doug was still up. Gordon knew Doug would get a kick out of his tale about his alleged brutality to the dummy.

He unlocked the door and stepped inside. Two half empty mugs sat on the coffee table. H'mmm, Stacey must have come home with Doug. But it wasn't like him not to clean up his mess.

Gordon turned toward the staircase. That was funny, a woman's shoe was on its side on the step. The matching one near the landing. Was that a blouse draped over the banister?

The faint murmur of voices floated downward. Gordon grinned, turned around and left.

* * *

"Is someone here?" Stacey raised herself up on her elbow. "I thought I heard something downstairs."

Doug caressed her arm. "It's probably Gordon. He has a knack for turning up at the wrong place at the wrong time. First thing in the morning, I'm telling him he's going to have to find a new place to live."

Stacey settled back into Doug's arms. "I knew I made the right decision the minute I saw your expression when I told you my answer was yes."

She smoothed his hair back from his brow, smiling momentarily before kissing him again. "I love you, Doug."

His grin was luminous in the darkened room. He kissed the palm of her hand. "I love you, Stacey."

About the Author

F. M. Meredith's first home was in a neighborhood filled with police officers and their families. She saw first hand how the job affected the families and the family affected the job, something she hopes she's portrayed in the Rocky Bluff P.D. series. When her son-in-law became a policeman, he added to her interest by telling her stories and taking her on a ride-along. More ride-along with male and female officers have added to her store of knowledge.

As a member of the Public Safety Writers Association, she's made many friends in law enforcement.

Meredith is a member of four chapters of Sisters in Crime, Mystery Writers of America, PSWA, Writers of Kern and Epic.

Printed in the United States
136469LV00002B/5/P

9 781892 343550